The End of Dreams

BRUCE GRAHAM

PURPLE PORCUPINE
PUBLISHING

First Published by Purple Porcupine Publishing
Copyright © 2021 Bruce Graham
All rights reserved.
ISBN: 978-1-7778211-3-5

This novel is entirely a work of fiction. The names, characters and incidents portrayed in it are the work of the author's imagination. Any resemblance to actual persons, living or dead, events or localities is entirely coincidental.

First Edition

For Sheila, Sister-in-law and friend.

Table of Contents

Preface

The End of Dreams was born through my interest in the history of both my family, and the American Civil War. Nova Scotians fought in the Civil War, and graveyards in my province contain veterans from both sides. Families lost sons; spies were everywhere in Halifax. Merchandise, illegal under U.S. Federal law, left ports along the Nova Scotia coast for starving Confederate hands. It was dangerous, but there was money to be made.

One of my maternal ancestors served in a Connecticut regiment during Civil War. Like many families before and after the early eighteenth century, my ancestors immigrated to Nova Scotia from Scotland. They had large families, as was the custom. Many of those children drifted in and out of the United States. My father was in the Connecticut Home Guard in World War One and worked in an ice plant in Florida. His brother became a preacher in New England. While my father returned to Nova Scotia, his brother stayed.

The End of Dreams evolved from another novel I started but never finished, called The West Wind and Me. It was planned as a multi-generational story told by an old house over two hundred years. The imaginary house is special to me because it is located on Kirk Hill near Parrsboro, Nova Scotia where my great grandparents farmed. In that story, two children who were kind to the house, many weren't, were Meredith and Liam McBurnie, the main characters in this book. Turns out I became more interested in them than the house. Around the same time, I was traveling and on the battlefield in Gettysburg. When I visited the museum there, I saw a clock on display that an army soldier had stolen and ideas collided and expanded.

As with most of my books, a woman, in this case, Meredith, is the protagonist. I find women more fascinating than men. Women have ego, but not male ego, which makes a tremendous difference in how life matters are handled. Women face up to things while men often choose to turn their heads away. In The End of Dreams, Meredith's journey is filled with challenges, but she is persistent and faces each one head-on with determination.

In my opinion, the bond that develops between writer and reader must give the reader some credit and some leeway in seeing the story through their own eyes. I hope you enjoy the book as much as I enjoyed writing it. I would encourage you to leave a review, as I am most interested in reading your thoughts about the book.

Prologue

The End of Dreams is a story of love and loss. It is about relationships between a brother and sister and a more fragile bond between mother and daughter. The women are at the core of this tale. The friction between them drove the daughter away as it had driven her brother, Liam. Meredith MacBurnie had experienced the slow decline in her mother. It began the day of the lightning. She had observed her mother change a little more year by year. Suddenly, due to a telegram, there is a new crisis. If the eldest daughter refused to chase after a missing brother who had deserted the Union Army, who might be sent to do their mother's bidding? Meredith was constantly harangued to do something.

Liam, the fair-haired boy, had not been heard from in fifteen months. He deserted, and Meredith has been sent to find him. The mission is impossible; the journey is dangerous. She has spent the past year working for a literary magazine in the New England States. Her employers urged her not to go, but if she must undertake such a foolhardy mission, write about it. Write everything. After all, Meredith dreams of being a writer.

There are a cast of characters Meredith meets in her search, including a homesick lieutenant and a one-footed soldier in Falmouth, Virginia, where she learns to drink sherry. Then the battlefields and destroyed farms and the hollow-eyed children of the homeless, freed slaves wandering the roads and deserters from both armies. Her journey is six hundred miles overland by wagon train to Nashville, Tennessee, a bustling Confederate town under Union control. She is employed by a potter, where she learned the streets of Nashville. Then she receives a position with a European doctor, who hires her to write a book about himself. In her search for stories, she befriends a sick and dying Tennessee prostitute and is shaken by the sorted things she hears.

Her brother is nowhere to be found. She is discouraged in Memphis, but things change in Kansas City, where against all odds, and because of her brother's talent with a graphite and sketch pad, Meredith gets an emotional jolt when Liam's artwork is on a poster in a store window.

She may be close on his trail, but the price for her search has been steep. There is violence everywhere, including the butchery of a newfound friend on the wagon train. Her ex-army traveling companion is murdered in front of her. Meredith does not escape personal violence. She is assaulted and found near death in the woods by a runaway slave girl.

If she finds him, Meredith wants them to return to their home in Nova Scotia. It was his leaving the farm that brought her family and her mother into the most violent state of nervous exhaustion. Maybe it will make things right if she can find him and bring him home. To make peace with his parents and to get to know his brothers and sisters. It is her best effort to reunite them all. What's a daughter to?

Chapter 1

The Rappahannock River
Virginia, 1864.

They were close, someone said, less than an hour from their destination. Meredith stood with a small group of men and women clustered by the railing on the upper deck. She had hardly slept due to the discomfort and noise. Her night had been made worst by the fact army pickets nearly stepped on her during their inspections. The dozen people at the railing comprised two distinct groups, those with funds to purchase a stateroom and the few, like Meredith, who had slept under the stars. Besides her nestled among war supplies was a Polish family comprising several children and parents and an elderly Virginia couple whose home had been used by the army for many months and may have been destroyed. Also sleeping on the deck was a young lawyer who appeared down on his luck.

As their riverboat cut through the early morning mist and the group strained to make out images on the riverbanks, a lively conversation had begun on the most talked about subject in the United States: the war. The men did most of the talking, particularly the blustery pastor whose name was Helms. He was pointing in the direction of Fredericksburg, where Federal forces had taken a real shellacking two years prior. The pastors' gleeful tone over the defeat of the United States Army would be considered treasonous in such places as Boston but not in Confederate Virginia, which had raised a massive army for the rebellion.

"Our boys will win it all," an older, plump woman declared, and her female companion nodded vigorously. Meredith standing behind them, said nothing.

"We have had our reversals," the Pastor Helms continued, *"but General Lee will march into Washington yet."*

The youthful lawyer, whose name was Edward Foley, had introduced himself when they boarded in Baltimore. He echoed a slightly different sentiment, *"War has torn us apart. Why cannot those in Washington let us live in peace? The waste in lives, the awful human waste."*

"And property too. Our home, I pray it will be still standing." declared a woman whom the pastor called Mrs. Howe.

"The Confederacy will be ultimately victorious," someone else vigorously declared, and there were several who voiced their agreement. Meredith thought differently. In her youthful but astute observation, time was running out for the Confederacy. The north controlled Baltimore, most of Virginia, the Tennessee River, and New Orleans. Had not General Sherman marched right through the state of Georgia. Most of the south was under Federal control. Meredith was surprised that there was still trade between the enemies despite three savage years of bloodshed between north and south. After all, as she had been told in Baltimore, business was business.

The crew on the riverboat were northerners. No confederate got a job transporting freight for the Union army unless it was contraband, and God knows there was plenty of that. The old riverboat had been boarded twice during the night by Federal pickets stationed along the Rappahannock. A half-hour stop each time, but it was more a social chat than a military inspection. There were inquiries about home folks and rather rakish jokes about women and condemnation of the war but no search, let alone seizure.

The passengers could not get breakfast as the dining room had been converted to stow freight for the U.S. Army. What could not be stowed in the dining room was piled on the deck. Replacement wheels for cannon limbers, salt beef, medicines, barrels of flour, and kegs of nails. It was more a floating freight barge than a passenger craft.

The *Pride of Baltimore* was old and battered with gouges and dents on its bulkheads; the railing was missing on the lower aft deck. Fingers of rust crawled up its stacks. Quickly snatched from the scrapyard and pressed into military service, there was little comparison to the majestic river queens that, before the war, had plied the waters of the Mississippi.

In Baltimore, Edward Foley had immediately noticed Meredith. She was young, hardly more than a girl. She was tall and beautiful with high cheekbones and flaxen hair that tumbled down her back. He knew this young woman had observed his frayed coat but introduced himself anyway with a short bow and tip of his hat. His boots were too run down for him to click his heels. None the less he tried to be a gentleman when they had boarded. They both slept on the deck twenty feet from each other with only barrels, bundles, and the Polish family between them. As she looked at him standing in the group, he attempted to restrain a huge yawn and excused himself with a weak smile. More people joined the group. They were mostly from the lower deck where they were supposed to remain, but it was wartime, and who did what they were told? After an uncomfortable night, people were walking about to get some feeling back in their feet and ward off the chill of the thick mist. The stateroom passengers were able to leave the riverboat first. They were in a particular hurry to do so now that the riff-raft from below was closing in on them. Irish immigrants were bad enough, but Yankee sailors and former slaves in military uniform? It was evident the appearance of black faces in blue uniforms jarred the confederates. The former slaves in the United States Army had learned to fight too and fight well. Pastor Helms ignored them and addressed a lady near him as Mrs. Taylor. She spoke for all to hear, caring not a bit about the soldiers. Her words were harsh, describing the swine, the cheats, and carpetbaggers picking over the bones of her charming southern home. Mrs. Taylor was thin of face with narrow shoulders. She was wrapped in a white shawl which she hugged tightly around herself. Her voice had the pitch and metallic twang of her southern roots.

"If Jefferson Davies was doing his job, this war would be over by now." She had no love for the Confederate leadership.

Meredith thought people would be suspicious of strangers, but the Confederates spoke openly and were unafraid of what they said. They leveled blistering criticisms of Jeff Davis, just as northerners could not hold their tongues on Mr. Lincoln's obvious shortcomings. The internal chemistry of the group was changing by the minute. The pastor had suddenly gone quiet. Meredith noticed how the boasts of eventual victory subsided as more black soldiers came upon the perimeter of the group.

Complaints of war shortages became the new subject. Mutterings and complaints of what could and could not be found in the shops. The group learned the man standing next to the plump Mrs. Howe was her husband, and the man who had replaced Pastor Helms doing most of the talking was a Virginia businessman from Richmond named MacDonald. He was returning from England, and he told the gathering the British would not, under any circumstances, get involved in the war. That comment momentarily took the oxygen out of the Confederates. They stood silently, watching the mist slowly evaporate from the river. Eventually, when talk began again, they learned the couple named Taylor and Mr. And Mrs. Howe were returning to Fredericksburg to inspect the damage done to their homes.

The Union army, before being slaughtered on the battlefield, had sacked many houses in the community. Union soldiers breaking down doors, stealing what they wanted. Their neighbour's barn had been burned to the ground, and their own home, always a place of temperance, had been filled with ungodly intoxication, liquor bottles rolling on the floor. Mrs. Taylor described it as a drunken orgy. She let out a deep sigh and declared her home had been turned into a place of degradation.

"The smell of Yankee vomit has permeated the walls, and there are no servants. They had all run off. Who is there to make things right again?"

Mrs. Howe said it was so uncomfortable living with northern relatives, and she and her husband could stand it no longer. It was difficult to live with someone and not talk about the war or worry aloud when there was so much to worry about. She hated being in the same room with her relatives when they had a silent celebration because the newspaper carried stories of a victory for the Union army or the sinking of a Confederate ship.

"They tried to be gracious, but my sister was clearly happy with our defeat, and her husband could not stop his smirk. It was too much," she said. *"I only hope our house is still standing."*

Pastor Helms spoke up again, stating that the Rappahannock River was close to the dividing line between north and south. What he did not say, but what they all knew was that since Mr. Lincoln's Emancipation, the focus of the conflict had shifted. The Rappahannock was now, for millions, the line between slavery and freedom.

In the first years of the war, the Confederacy had won many battles. But it was now in a spiraling death struggle. The southern economy was shot. Thousands of Confederate soldiers deserted, many rushing home to protect their families. There were bread riots in Richmond, the Confederate capital.

Meredith ran her hand through her hair and tried not to appear interested in what was said. She had no intention of revealing the fact her residency in the United States had existed less than a year. Yet, she was astonished at some of the things she heard. The optimistic comments being spoken in the early morning mist were primarily delusional. Since leaving Maine, Meredith McBurnie had witnessed the strength of the United States Army and the men and munitions ready for shipment. The troops and stockpiles in Boston, New York, and Washington, to say nothing of the flourishing port of Baltimore. So many cannon, and ships and soldiers: who could stand against such force? The war was grinding on in its fourth endless year. And it was easy to detect the distress and bitterness in her small group. She noticed, despite comments otherwise, the hard lines on the faces of those around her and the distant sadness in their war-weary eyes. Mrs. Howe was silently weeping. A sudden lull had taken hold of the conversation as if the unsaid truth was eating away at the former notes of victory.

Silently, they watched the half-concealed riverbanks glide by. The sun was cutting through the thick mist of early morning, revealing an occasional outline of a rustic cabin or a small farmhouse with a cobbled-together barn. The ill-defined images and obscure shapes formed an unfinished painting: eerie yet beautiful in its half-revealed serenity. The less obscured landscape slumbered past soundless except for the hard throb of the steam engine and the occasional squawk of a long-legged river bird disturbed from its hunting. Flotsam filled the edges of the river with straws and sticks and once or twice what looked like pieces of clothing, a sleeve, or a cap. Other items bobbed on the surface that they could not identify.

The riverboat had taken them from Baltimore down the frothy chop of the Chesapeake Bay with its brackish waters. Then their craft cut sharply into the Rappahannock, that meandering inland waterway that penetrates the soft soil of

Virginia like a hot knife, rolling inland almost two hundred miles giving passengers a transitory sketch of green pastures wrested from the frontier. The gnarled woods had been tamed by early settlers. The cultivation revealed the years of the hard work of many men and women replacing thick forests with orchards of peach and apples and gardens of corn and cotton. What the passengers could see of the farms was strange: no cattle, hogs, geese, or ducks were in evidence. The river flowed through rural stillness into two-bit hamlets with rickety docks hardly big enough for a donkey cart. There were more prized communities downstream with real waterfronts, warehouses, and wharves. But what they saw was an empty land. The early morning mist rose in smoky puffs disappearing in the dawn of a new day as more of the surrounding country revealed itself. It was spring in Virginia, and despite the early hour, the sun was becoming strong. Odd-shaped shadows on the riverbanks obscured only minutes earlier were now visible.

There were spots where it is obvious the war had come and gone. All that remained were gouges in the ground, the result of twelve-pound cannonballs, the pastor said, and no one disagreed. They came upon upright girders, the remains of a bridge standing erect in the river. Meredith would later write the iron girders had a defiant manner about them as if stating - I am strong, and I will be rebuilt. The battered barges resting on the riverbank gave no such impression. Significant gaps in their hulls told of their total desolation. What was missing was the blood-curdling cries of the terrified and the exhausted, the clash of bayonets and crack of musket fire. All was quiet on this ghostly morning: no braying of dying horses or curses of murderous men.

Meredith McBurnie was a novice to battlefields and bloodshed. She was a farm girl and had seen animals give birth and was familiar with their slaughter. At thirteen, she was aware of what it was when her monthlies began; otherwise, outside the farm, the bloodiest thing she had to contend with was when one of her students broke his nose and bled all over her. She had never heard the homicidal roar of a cannonball, nor the killer rush of its air, so close to your ear your head ached for days. But her imagination was both vivid and strong. She read and thought she knew the workings of things. But the vibration of one's insides when a murderous projectile roars near your skin was beyond her. She had never heard the tremendous tearing artillery makes in the fabric of an advancing army, nor did she quite see the rock and topsoil ripped from the earth and hurled maddeningly skyward only to rain down again as a muddy, rocky shower covering men and horses: the living and the dead. Such things happened on that very riverbank at that destroyed bridge.

Meredith did understand they are close to the location where young men died by the thousands, and many who didn't die shit themselves in dire fright while charging into battle. She knew they were close to where men had gone mad or permanently deaf: the impact of cannon snapping eardrums like eggshells. When the black soldiers, as bored as the rest of them, moved away from the group, the bluster began again. The burly businessman MacDonald was trying to outperform Pastor Helms in condemning everything Yankee. Meredith concentrated on the landscape. She was letting her imagination run away with her as she tried to visualize the screams, the cannon fire, the drums and the crack of fire-repeating rifles, and the smoky belch of old Flintlocks. The music of war was playing in her mind: the rumble of a phantasmal symphony.

Rounding the bend, the riverboat let go a blast from its steam horn, sending screeching ravens skyward from the overhanging willows. Meredith was excited and scared as she prepared to move into a world she did not know. She was eighteen years old. A schoolteacher for only one term. A young woman who could imagine anything and everything. A seeker of adventure who left her Nova Scotia home for a literary position in Maine. From Portland to Boston and New York and on to Washington and Baltimore, there had been plenty to see. There were trampled fields where great armies had recently camped. The war had moved beyond her, yet the apprehension of her mission began to envelop her as the river mist had done during the night. She was near the beginning of her search.

Meredith had seven letters in her possession. One pressed flat and nicely folded was from her employers as a way of introduction, acknowledging her honesty and all-around good character. Lewis Clark didn't want to write that letter. He almost had to have a gun held to his head for him to take up pen and paper, all the time telling her she was mad to go off on such a venture that would bring her both heartache and great personal peril. His wife Clarissa was the one holding the gun. She had been more sympathetic and understanding of the great dilemma their newest employee faced.

Lewis's letter was to be presented when needed. The other letters were not for public presentation. One was from her brother Liam, telling her things that greatly alarmed her. His words were powerful, espousing the shocking emotion of his near-death experience. He described the event in vivid detail as only a poet could. The other five letters were crumpled into balls to be discarded but had not been thrown away. The last three were close to the ranting of a madwoman. A woman Meredith feared her mother was becoming. It churned in Meredith's mind like an auger. In obeying the pleadings of her mother, was she acting in a rational manner? Meredith knew part of it was guilt. Her guilt for rejecting her mother's wishes that she remain at home and continue as a schoolteacher. Vena made it very clear Meredith should feel guilty for abandoning her parents as Liam had done. But instead of backtracking to her family in Nova Scotia to offer solace of some sort, she was going in the other direction into the Confederate States of America. It was a land dripping in the blood of hundreds of thousands of devoured men, many the age of herself and her brothers.

Meredith turned towards the east and let the rising sunbathe her face. The riverboat rounded another corner, and the vanishing mist granted her the first real glimpse of a grisly aftermath of combat. There it was before her: wars' residue. The scarred and pocked landscape with half-collapsed buildings, broken walls, and uprooted trees. All conversation around her stopped as the passengers stood transfixed. The war had come to the Rappahannock in its second year. Already weeds, saplings, wild daisies, and joy bells were doing their best to conceal the scars of the landscape. There was a gasp, from someone. A groan from Mrs. Howe. Her husband embraced her.

"*Dear God, help us.*" Someone whispered.

"*Traveling alone, Miss?*" Edward Foley had asked Meredith in Baltimore. She lied to him, "*I am visiting my aunt in Falmouth.*"

A short blast of the steam whistle. They were pulling into a tattered and torn community that was her destination. They had all gone quiet. Even the pastor had stopped talking as everyone's attention was suddenly on the bedlam below as the riverboat drew into to the dock. The waterfront was sheer pandemonium. The anguished cries of cattle and the crackle of the whips as the drovers attempted to push their animals into a tighter and tighter knot onto the wharf. A hectic flock of geese were complaining loudly but minding the two barking dogs guarding them. Behind the cattle were carts and horses. Men were arguing, their horses braying made nervous by the cattle and geese and barking dogs and rough words. Everything was crowded in confusion, particularly since the Federal soldiers had blocked off one side of the narrow wharf, making things extremely noisy and congested. The scene was accompanied by a nauseating pungent aroma as if a stinking veil had been thrown over the passengers. The stench was human: of unwashed men. Meredith could see them standing in a long line. Bedraggled Confederate prisoners-of-war waiting to be sent somewhere. Falmouth was a transport depot for prisoners captured by the United States army; Meredith had read as much. But such a close encounter upon her arrival. She was not prepared for such an experience.

The prisoners, two by two, with their coughs, bandages, and crutches made a line along one side of the bustling dock. A very few at the front were restrained by chains. Most were restrained by hunger and ill health. They were lined up as if preparing to march: a parade of the grimy-faced and blood-stained. Muskets were replaced by wooden crutches; bright uniforms traded for bloody bandages. They were the antithesis of what they had been. When marching off to war they were clean-faced soldiers, untested but with chests full of pride. Their boots and brass buttons polished. Cheering was ringing in their ears. How deeply they drank the ovation of the noisy crowds. Military music mingled with applause. The glory of it. The great adventure awaited them.

Meredith did not leave the railing; she wanted to capture the scene in her mind, to recall it later. Concentrate on everything. There was a story here. Something the Clark's could use. The prisoners were two abreast, with every twenty or so guarded by a Union soldier who appeared as bored as the prisoners. They did not seem to have the will to escape. The sunken faces of the starving said they were beyond such endeavors. It was harsh to say, but these men were the losers, not only in their military conflict but almost certainly, contrary to the pastor's opinion, the losers in the larger national all-encompassing struggle. After early success, their great rebellion was backfiring. With thinking people, it was understood by 1864 that the north would win. Unless, of course, there was some unlikely miracle in the state of Tennessee. Some still believed in miracles.

With portmanteau securely in hand and bedroll over her shoulder Meredith waited for the others to leave. Then she quickly descended to the main deck and down the gangplank into the noise and bedlam of braying cattle mixed with the obscene cursing of the drovers as if there were not a Christian soul in miles. Freight wagons bumped each other trying to get ahead of the cattle and as close as possible to the riverboat to load their cargo and be gone. Edward Foley hurried ahead of her with a man Meredith had not seen before. The man was tightly grasping Folly's arm as if he might fly away or try to escape. The disembarking passengers were forced to walk very close to the confederate prisoners: no more than an arm's length away.

Meredith felt a thousand eyes on her. *"I am on display."* She thought.

"Get your head up and your shoulders straight!" Her mother's harsh words suddenly ringing in her ears. But she did as she was told.

Despite the clamorous and crowded conditions as she passed down the line, Meredith received salutations from more than one of the prisoners. Mr. And Mrs. Howe were ahead of her and clutching each other, hesitating while gaping awestruck at the general dilapidation of the prisoners. The young lawyer in the frayed coat and the man clutching his arm disappeared in the crowd.

Directly ahead of her, Mrs. Taylor was sobbing. *"It is all too much,"* she said to Pastor Helms, *"to look at these boys who had fought for us. God bless you, my sons,"* she called out to them, *"you will not be forgotten. God bless you."*

Without warning a young soldier spoke to Meredith, *"And God bless you, Mam."* Meredith was startled but didn't stop or catch his face.

Mrs. Taylor was soliciting comments from the prisoners while just ahead, Mrs. Howe faltered in her step and was heavily supported by her husband. There were other comments from all directions but could not be fully heard above the clamor, made worse because some of the geese had escaped the vigilance of the dogs and were suddenly running among the legs of the cattle. The drovers reared their mounts, attempting to use the horse's hoofs to stamp on the birds. A fight broke out, and people stopped to watch the fisticuffs. Meredith did not. A young prisoner of war, hardly more than a boy, smiled before she got to him. She felt it unsettling to be smiled at by a face with one eye missing. *"Hello,"* was all he said. Meredith took a deep breath and looked him straight in his eye and offered a weak smile, then nodded before the guard roughly told her to move along.

"Move along?" There was no intention of stopping to chat. She suddenly felt dizzy. Dear God, they hadn't bathed. Dried blood masked many uniforms. Soiled garments bore the stains of injury and suffering. These men needed tending. Some of the prisoners were gesticulating, holding a personal conversation in the midst of the madness. They spoke to no one in particular about the crops, the farm, and subjects unrelated to the war. One or two were ranting loudly, adding to the frenzy around them. They cried out on the whereabouts of their family. One declared, loudly, that Jesus would destroy the godless northern army. *"Have no fear, friends. Jesus will save us. Do not lose your faith, my fellows."*

The guards appeared to care for nothing. They made no attempt to break up the fistfight that had stopped traffic, nor did they turn their attention to the noisy commotion behind them. They watched the prisoners in a state of total apathy and disinterest. The prisoners were moving along, obeying some unheard order to advance. They filed onto the riverboat to be delivered elsewhere to some new hell, worse perhaps than what they had recently endured.

Young Meredith McBurnie had briefly glimpsed the pock-marked landscapes, uprooted trees, and charred buildings. Now she was seeing the human carnage of flesh and bone. The line of men with their bandages and blood stood out in the glare of the suddenly intense morning sun that had burst forth in full radiance in the Virginia sky. The prisoners suddenly appeared bolder and brighter and their dissipation more intense and horrible in the full light of a Virginia morning.

Chapter 2

Despite the hectic activity on the dock, the dusty little hamlet of Falmouth looked deserted. It was war-worn and dilapidated as if the boots of a million men had tried to kick the boards out of every building. However, Falmouth had to be the place; there was no choice. For his family, for his friends, for the world at large, this is where Liam's story ended. Where else was there to begin?

All Meredith knew for certain was what Liam had written her. He had killed a man, not with his blue-coated Union buddies by his side as he had done during the raging battle in Fredericksburg. No, this fight was different. Solitary, without soldiers or drummers or cannon or the rattling of sabers or the sound of cavalry. This was a desolate experience, an extraordinary military conquest between two men. It took place on a dreary, darkened country road outside his camp. A single shadow had approached in the twilight. Liam thought it was one of his own until he knew it was a southern boy, as hungry and lost as he was.

Liam's regiment had been scattered and in retreat for twenty-four hours. War-weary to begin with, they had gone in a wide circle, staggering through woods and thickets. They walked for endless hours, separated from their main units or what was left of them. At one point, Liam was sure they had crossed the same stream seven hours earlier. He was right. They ended up almost back at the scene of the battle. A battle so ferocious that in the midst of it, his insides tightened until he could not get his breath. They were dispirited, exhausted, and starving. The Union army had lost a great battle, and many of his comrades and many others he did not know but wore a similar uniform lay dead on the battlefield. According to his sole letter, he had been foraging for firewood on his Sergeant's orders. He had lost his way and was standing at the edge of the darkened road with his arms full of sticks for the cooking fires. He was trying to decide which direction would take him back to his camp when he saw the lone silhouette approaching. Their first words to each other were cordial until they could distinguish the others' uniforms. The grays of the Confederate lads were ripped and dirty, Liam's, a little less so. But he had seen terrible bloodshed and human carnage that made him literally tremble for hours after. He was not a raw recruit.

The Confederate seemed shocked to come upon a Union soldier. He asked Liam why he wasn't at least in the next county, a hundred miles away after the whipping they had taken. Liam had no answer. He wondered as much himself. He wrote Meredith how relieved he was when the young man suddenly turned away as if retracing his steps. Then the Confederate halted and put his hands together and stood very still with his back to Liam. He appeared to be in prayer. Thunder made a slow, muffled rumble in the distance. The rain started, and chain lightning flashed on the horizon. Slowly the Confederate bent down and pulled a knife with a long blade from his boot. Turning, he declared in a solemn voice that he would never dishonor his father and grandfather, who were counting on him. The entire south was counting on him.

The youthful man slowly approached Liam, who dropped his sticks except the heaviest one, which he held tightly. They crouched menacingly, circling each other. The rain came harder, and with it thunder. The Confederate waved his knife. Liam held his stick in a defensive position. As they moved around each other looking for an advantage, the Confederate explained in a low southern drawl that he had sworn an oath on the family Bible, never to run from a fight. Liam tried to placate his adversary, saying they could walk away from each other. They need not fight the war by themselves. The confederate boy was having none of it. As they circled each other, Liam understood he was in for the fight of his life. Clutching his stick and wiping the rain from his face, he tried again to convince the young man that they could simply walk away. Let the armies fight the war. When the Confederate declared his ancestors were looking down on him in this hour of struggle. Liam felt disgust, the same anger he had experienced in battle, the same tightening in his chest as in the final hours at Fredericksburg. With his friends dead in the field and so many others, in such numbers, a great rage came over him. His regiment had attacked the Confederates time after time until the ground was littered with bodies. He looked around at the carnage and felt the rage that fully seized him in its grasp. At that moment facing his lone opponent, he cursed and told the Confederate he need not worry as his ancestors had burnt to a crisp in the fires of hell long ago. They spent minutes uttering such insults as the rain beat down. *"A Dance of Death"* was how Liam described it. An intense, truly awful physical struggle, and only one of them would survive. More than once, lightning flashed on the blade of the knife as they circled each other. This was a deadly conflict of newly minted men, more ferocious because of the youthful adrenalin of abject terror.

Liam did not hesitate to describe the taste of fear as he felt the swish of the blade close to his face, the tightness in his chest, and how the acidity of panic burned in his mouth. He described how every muscle became brittle as if his limbs might fall from his body. He forgot his exhaustion and wrote the fear of dying was both invigorating and paralyzing. The Confederate repeatedly swung his blade with Liam's stick, his only offensive weapon. After one mighty swing, the Confederate was slightly off balance. Liam lunged and struck the man hard on the head with the firewood knocking him to the ground. In a split second, Liam was upon him. They struggled for the knife, and Liam raised the firewood and struck him again and again. Suddenly he had the knife in his hand, and he plunged it deeply.

In the morning, they went to find the lanky lad he had left by the edge of the road. It was Liam's first real look at his opponent's face. Dear God, he was a boy, maybe sixteen or seventeen. A good-looking boy, a sweet child, was how Liam described him. A sleeping child, except his breast was covered in blood. In his pocket was a half-written letter to his mother. The Sergeant ripped it up, saying he won't be finishing his correspondence, and the half dozen men in the detail laughed. Liam cringed. He wanted to write to the boy's mother and inform her what had happened. That he did not want to kill her son.

Meredith understood the deadly struggle that tore the soul out of her brother, even more than the slaughter of thousands at Fredericksburg. The solitary act of killing a man was not like war. Liam called it murder, and it was eating away at him as he told her how he had plunged the knife into the lad's chest, and there was a great moan and what Liam thought was the dying boy's last word - mother. That sound he said that final utterance would not leave him. It stayed in his ears.

Meredith cried as she read. It was so much like Liam: everything in great and vivid detail, even the dying gasp of his adversary and the shock, the profound impact of it. He had killed the man, reported the incident to his superiors, wrote a long, detailed letter to Meredith, a more condensed one to his parents, and in the middle of the next night, still shaken to his core Liam McBurnie deserted the United States Army.

How could she not cry? Was there ever a boy who less deserved to be a soldier? Liam, the poet, the musician, the artist. Vividly she pictured him on a warm summer afternoon with half a dozen of their friends. They had music and singing, and for another amusement, they made up poems. Liam's was always the best, the most heartfelt. Meredith sensed the others were playing at poetry, but her brother was doing something more. The last August afternoon when they were all together, and by then Jacob too. Already handsome, little brother Jacob was a heartthrob and had no trouble fitting into social gatherings. For their special occasions, they congregated at the edge of the plateau where they could look over the valley and the far-off church steeples of the town below. In front of friends, Meredith had not expected anything unusual. She certainly did not expect a poem dedicated to her. She remembered the pride and how it warmed her until the last line when her brother, in a full voice, said,

> "*the greatest gift God hath given me,*
> *is permitting the sinner that I be,*
> *to save my sister from the sea.*"

An unusual concoction of emotions rushed through Meredith that last afternoon: a mixture of shattered pride and rising embarrassment. She wanted to protest, to tell them it was not true. Liam had always taken credit for something that was false. Instead, she sat back and said nothing. She was lost to the other poems, but no one seemed to notice. The struggle within was hers alone. She watched him as he listened to the others with their mostly silly recitals, enjoying himself immensely. There was so much to her brother. Even at a young age, he could draw and sketch better than other children. He had mastered the flute: had taken it up as a tribute to Flora.

The memory of his music filling the farmyard, emanating from the nearby pines, was so clear and lovely it produced a pang in her heart.

Liam was small and not as handsome as Jacob but well-proportioned with broad shoulders. More cute than handsome with the same flaxen hair and a kind face. His brown eyes were intelligent and expressive. Liam could sing and was considered a good dancer. He had mastered the flute, with which he made beautiful music. He loved to sketch and loved cartooning.

Liam and Meredith had a special place they did not take the others. A small glade by the brook, fenced by pine trees on one side of the babbling water and a petite outcropping of rocks on the other side that made it very private. It was a place they called their own, and it was there Liam had laid out his life plans: a professional cartoonist for a newspaper. Music was his mistress, was how he had put it, but drawing was his delight. A delight to his friends as well when presented with a new caricature of themselves.

Liam had some detractors, such as the local pastor and once, the high sheriff of Cumberland County, who said Liam was intent on throwing his life away with cards and rough friends. He didn't shun farm work, but unlike Jacob, he didn't take to it either. Their father had taken ill in the winter and never fully recovered, and by rights, Liam should have run the farm.

Meredith and Liam retired to the glade whenever possible in those days, often to talk about their parents. Liam confided that he could see his future, and it was disastrous. He was being trapped. He had to escape. And escape he did. Within months he was gone. His departure was made more hastily by the family tension. Her mother had lost children and didn't want to lose Liam. Vena McBurnie had never been quite the same since the afternoon of the lightning. She was furious her son would abandon them. How inconsiderate! Unable to cope with her children or the hardships of life, Vena wanted to wrap her children around her in a protective cloak. Yet, it seemed to Meredith, her mother had also lost the ability to love. Vena was so fully and forcefully against Liam leaving that unintentionally, her actions rushed his departure. During the evening meals, she made dramatic scenes, rising from the table once, pointing her bone-thin, accusing finger at her son, and calling him a traitor for walking out on them with his father ill. Had they not always given him love and shelter.

Meredith tried to intervene on her brother's behalf and so had her father, but soft-spoken Clifton was shouted down, and Janet didn't help siding with her mother. Janet would always side against Meredith. The tension became unbearable. Liam was soon out the door leaving his mother wretched, furious, and sobbing.

He shipped out of the port of Parrsboro to Boston in hopes of securing employment. The war was in high gear, and jobs were plentiful. He found work in the masonry trade as a bricklayer's assistant. He soon proved himself very capable with his hands. Too capable, it turned out, creating resentment with his fellow workers until he was thrust onto the street. He was handy with a hammer too. He had helped his father with repairs to the farm buildings and pitched in at barn raisings. He got a job constructing a fine wooden and brick home on Commonwealth Ave, in the heart of Boston.

In 1863, after the Battle of Gettysburg, the economic climate changed. The war had begun to wind down. When the beautiful house was completed, there was no more work. Newspapers turned down his cartoons. They did not require his talents. Liam's future suddenly held less promise. Although he was never really a follower, he followed some of his new friends into the Union Army of the United States, 22nd Massachusetts Infantry. There was still a need for soldiers.

In his native Nova Scotia, the political and social climate in those years was also becoming heated, but with a much smaller charge than south of the border. It was more a war of ideas on what the future should look like: a merger of Nova Scotia, New Brunswick, and Prince Edward Isle was the talk. There were those who said young people should not run off to the United States, that the future in Nova Scotia was bright. There was clamorous debate and all sorts of yammering up and down the counties. Political union, they said, would bring jobs, and jobs would bring prosperity. Hallelujah.

By the time he was ready to leave, Liam was deaf to all such promises. His dreams were different. Everything about his character, talents, kind spirit and bravery made him the man he was and particularly contradictory to the two endeavors he had found himself waist-deep in - farming and war. His last year at home, he spent more of his time alone in the evergreens. Meredith could usually find him if she had a mind to. He had his special places, under a big pine or propped up on the warm rocks above the little brook.

Meredith and Liam confided in each other. They were in their own sphere of influence: closer in age and spirit than the other children. Liam told Meredith neither he nor she needed to remain: their siblings were coming of age. "I see Jacob taking over the farm. He has the aptitude for it."

Liam wanted to inspect the great galleries of the world: the famous museums that other countries possessed, but his hollow, empty land did not yet have. He wanted to sell his cartoons and characterizations to big-city newspapers. Liam had dreams, big dreams.

When the news of her son's desertion reached the farm, Vena McBurnie opened her front door on a stormy Nova Scotia night and howled with such force, her baleful complaint could be heard on the next farm. Leaving home was bad enough. Going into the army was worse. Now, this new hell. Desertion meant he was fair game to be shot by either side.

Awoken by her howl, a very alarmed Clifton and the children found the front door wide open and Vena on her hands and knees, the fury burnt out of her. The crumpled one-line notification from the United States Army was still clutched in her fingers. Life at home was hell after that. Meredith missed the worst of it. She was already gone by then. When her teaching term was over, filled with angst, regret, and humiliation, she had followed Liam out the door. She was gone before word came he had joined the army, and well before that troubling telegram arrived that was twisting like a knife in the family. The telegram curtly announced Liam was a deserter. If he showed himself, his parents had a legal obligation to turn him over to authorities. Meredith wondered if the army understood that Nova Scotia was not part of the United States, although many people on both sides of the border wished it to be.

When Vena regained her strength, she started a strenuous letter-writing campaign that dwarfed all other crusades launched by desperate mothers. That one woman could be the author of so many epistles and appeals for assistance was truly astonishing. Each day before he opened his cobbler shop on Parrsboro's Main Street, Clifton McBurnie made his daily trek across the street to the town's post office. But who could help a deserter in a foreign war? Dr. Tupper, a man of politics and great significance, told her bluntly,

"The United States is in no mood to take direction or offer assistance to Nova Scotia when its principal city is full of spies, people like our dear Mr. Keith and his corrupted bunch working for the confederacy."

Officialdom could do nothing. The only assistance possible was from members of her own family. That's when the showers of letters began to rain down on Meredith. They came one or two a week just as she was getting settled in her new position as proofreader and assistant to the editor at the New England Journal.

While Meredith resisted, Vena gave her daughter a clear choice: *"find my son or come home and look after our family so I can shoulder the task myself."*

Then she threw in the added jab. That big lie that her family believed and that Liam had constantly promoted and Meredith had never denied. It stung the most.

"After all, you owe him your life."

The weekly shower of letters became a torrent. A new missive slapped down on her desk each morning. The men on staff joked about her fan mail. *"Letters from beaus. Is it dear?"* But Clarissa Clark could see how morally and physically wounded and beaten down her new employee was becoming upon reading, day after day, her mother's rants.

"Have I not suffered enough? Has my life not been filled with every disappointment? The hardship I endure. The farm which is paying us nothing. Your father's health gets worst, Liam and you running off. Jacob is going with a scruff from town and will not leave her alone. Janet has taken up with a man I do not approve of. Sarah is mad and thinks nothing of taking off her clothes in front of strangers. She needs me watching her every minute."

It was impossible to find Liam, Meredith told her mother, over and over in letter after letter. A fools' errand. She knew it; everyone knew it. Where would I start to look? He could be anywhere in the United States or anywhere in the world.

Meredith understood the role she played in her mother's disappointment. Certainly, she had not really wanted to be a school teacher but let herself be bullied, first by her mother, then persuaded by the school trustees that instructing youngsters was of the highest order: a lofty profession where the reward was self-satisfaction in the knowledge of good work. Rich words for a position that paid a pittance.

Meredith had regretted her teaching decision almost immediately. It was not her calling. The children she loved she cared for too much, wanting to take them to her bosom, but there was no compulsion to bring the slow learners along, no challenge to her finer instincts. She was not cut out to be a teacher. A month into her position, the school trustees were informed she would only remain for one term. Violating her contract was a black mark against her character, they told her.

"Then I will have to carry that mark with me."

Without Liam, it was worse at home. Meredith had lost her kindred spirit. Jacob and the twins tried to fill the gap. Her sisters were brutal. Sarah would never be right, and Janet, it seemed, would never be happy. Only her dear father had kept her there, but with teaching over, Meredith longed to go. There was more to life than living on a plateau above a little town in Nova Scotia, waiting to marry some country clodhopper. Her father, Clifton, was a kind and gentle man, but Meredith's relationship with her mother was strained. Since what happened to Flora, her mother had stopped what little affection she ever offered to Meredith, replacing warmth with constant criticism. In turn, Meredith gave everything she could to her siblings. She didn't want a life of looking after children as the oldest daughter she already had enough of that. Astute enough to understand the drudgery and meager existence of a farm wife, Meredith saw it every morning, passing hardscrabble farms on the way to her school traveling down from the plateau and into town with her father.

As Meredith walked away from the incredible commotion of the dock in the small Virginia hamlet of Falmouth, an unidentified soldier was suddenly beside her. She wasn't sure where he had come from. Despite the commotion, she had been walking through or maybe as a way of overcoming it, her thoughts were very far away. In her minds-eye, she had been imagining her father dutifully taking his wife's latest correspondence to the post office. It made her want to weep. She had found her calling only to put it aside for this impossible search: this crazy mission.

When her true calling was finally found, it was quite by accident. The war in the United States was much talked about in Nova Scotia. It had made some of the wily local sea captains quite rich. Smuggling, blockade running, carrying arms, ammunition. Men with ambition and daring took to the sea for wealth, showing little concern for the consequences. The war was causing social changes as well. An article on the suffragettes in a New England literary magazine had deeply offended Meredith. She fumed for a day and then wrote the publication a blistering response. It felt good when she penned it despite the fact, she considered it discourteous and unpleasant. To her surprise, they published it.

Her reaction to being published evolved in stages. First, she was stunned, then angry at their liberty in making public her words, then embarrassed at her vehemence. And when all that was done, she was surprised and pleased when Lewis Clark, the editor, wrote a short note saying the response to her letter had stirred a great deal of attention and feedback. The publisher encouraged "M. McBurnie" to comment on whatever subject he desired with the same irascible eloquence he provided their readers in the April issue. The magazine was The *New England Journal* out of Portland, Maine. The publication was a rare combination of northeast rural New England folksiness and Bostonian high-minded literary pretensions with many famous contributors to its Editors Table, including Longfellow and Oliver Wendell Holmes. Publishers Lewis and Clarissa Clark saw it as their mandate to encourage new talent. They saw in M. McBurnie's writing a force and passion they admired. However, her subsequent five offerings on a variety of observations that encompassed a great deal of her time and effort disappointingly were not published. She went back over her initial offering and saw the difference. Her first and only published piece had been so passionate, angry, and certain of the point of view expressed. The words were her weapons, and it came to Meredith. They didn't want honest opinions from ordinary citizens. They wanted the flaming issuance of a lunatic. She wrote and told them as much. Thus began a series of correspondence between Lewis Clark and Meredith that led, months later, to a job offer.

M. McBurnie accepted.

Imagine how surprised Lewis Clark was when a fair female, a comely lass of the tender age of eighteen years turned up as M. McBurnie. If Mr. Clark's eyebrows could have gone any higher, they would have settled on his hairline. For an editor, a man of words, he had extreme difficulty putting a sentence together. After a few faltering starts he blurted out,

"We, we don't have women working here…"

"So, I'll be your first then."

"Yes, well no, not really."

"Please explained yourself, Mr. Clark"

"Well, ah, we're not geared up for women."

"What gear do you require?"

"Well, a,..a we, we only have one toilet er, ah water closet, to a, use, you see."

"I will promise not to leave it in an unsightly condition."

This was a showdown, and she was prepared to stand her ground. She was not going home. He had offered M. McBurnie a trial position. She was here to collect on his offer. He tried to be adamant, at one point playing the tough newspaper editor. Meredith was unmoved. She refused to leave when he ordered her to.

"You will have to throw me out physically, and I warn you, I am a farm girl, and I can scrap when I have to."

"Dear Lord, young lady I have no intention of doing that."

People came in and out of his office giving her odd looks and sideways glances and once or twice an encouraging smile. One old gentleman whispered as he passed her, *"Wear him down, darling, you can do it."*

Then everything changed. A new arrival marched into the field of battle. Co-publisher Clarissa Clark stormed into the cluttered office and after setting her sights on Meredith, turned to her husband.

"You cannot bring someone in here on a job offer and then refuse them the job, really Lewis, what are you thinking?"

Both women were standing in front of him, staring down as all Clark could do was fumble with some object on his desk as if it was the biggest bother he currently faced. Before Mrs. Clark's arrival, Meredith had already twice refused to leave. With her new ally, they soon overtook him: two Gothic statues with fixed eyes and nostrils flaring. Meredith McBurnie secured the promised position.

It was mostly editing what other people wrote, correspondents from northern Maine and Vermont, volunteers who wrote a column a month and needed her sharp eye to chase down improper pronouns and inactive verbs. The Clark's themselves worked on the big names, for certain Meredith was not editing Walt Whitman. They were a good team, Lewis was the intellectual, Clarissa the practical manager. She ran the business; he did the writing and heavy editing. It had been only seven months later when Meredith, trying to hold back the tears, tendered her resignation.

Both Lewis and Clarissa tried to persuade Meredith to change her mind and stay. One evening after a farewell dinner at their home, she broke down and showed them the letter from Liam as well as her mother's rambling correspondence. The Clark's looked at her in dismay. The conversation and reading, and discussion of the letters lasted hours. They at least understood why she was leaving the job she loved. It drew them closer to her. That night Lewis and Clarissa Clark became not just employers but fast friends.

"If you're determined to do this. Write the story of it. Make your travel something people can sink their teeth into. You have the talent. If you must go, make it mean something."

Reluctant to write about her brother, they agreed she would write about the war and the people she came upon during her travels.

"And you know, when this is over, you are welcome back," Clarissa added.

Just weeks later, she was passing prisoners-of-war, and some were being rude, whispering, *"Pretty miss, how bout given' us a kiss."* A few abbreviated laughs then silence as they returned to their subdued manner. She was finally past them. The prisoners, the cattle, horses, droves, and dogs were behind her. The soldier who came out of nowhere was still striding quietly beside her. She took a deep breath.

Her quest had begun.

Chapter 3

The main street of Falmouth was dusty and deserted. Cannon fire would hit nothing but a mangy dog or two. Great armies had been and gone. The stars and stripes had replaced the Confederate flag. U. S. military law ruled. Meredith hesitated, uncertain of which way to go, and turned to the lanky soldier who had taken alongside her. The group from the riverboat were dispersing just ahead, but this soldier had kept abreast of her. He had a slight hitch to his walk, and he halted when she stopped. He was young, slightly taller than her, with deep-set eyes. Meredith asked where she could find the people in charge. He said he would take her to his commanding officer.

"*Show you the way, as the preachers say,*" and he let out a guffaw and chortle that made her smile. The army camp was a short distance away from the river, and every flap on every tent was open. The tents were empty. Several women were working over washing tubs, and a half dozen soldiers were playing cards under a Magnolia tree, their shirts off, their long johns, unbuttoned to the waist. It promised to be a very warm day. The atmosphere surprised her. It was too relaxed. There was no marching, no guards, and hardly any soldiers except for the card players. The young private explained that the army was in another part of the state. So was the general and second and third in command; they were all joining up to move west. The Lieutenant was in charge for the time being. The soldier had a boyish manner about him. He never seemed to take his eyes off Meredith as they walked through the tents. A few minutes later, he pointed to the only wooden building in the midst of the sea of white canvas. The rough log cabin with its low-slung roof already radiated heat. She knew it would be an oven inside. A dark oven at that, with only one window and the sooty tang of smoky lantern oil and tobacco juice. Until her eyes adjusted, the man behind the desk appeared as a lump of jelly. When he could be finally seen, Meredith sensed immediately that he was not a professional soldier. The army was full of men who didn't graduate from West Point. Citizen soldiers came from all ranks and walks of life. Volunteers with military training rushed. As the war had dragged on, many of the professionals had been killed on the battlefields. Many more felled by disease.

Her eyes did not deceive her. The man across the desk was lumpy and appeared rather uncomfortable in her presence. Whatever his pain, it certainly wasn't hunger. This man was burly. The type of man who had never gone hungry. His big eyes were downtrodden, and she wondered how a man with such a hound-dog countenance had been left in charge of anything. He could not take charge of his own hair with tufts pointing in several directions. He appeared to be in need of re-arranging as if his entire demeanor, as well as his clothing, were somehow askew. Even the scar on his cheek needed fixing. On another face it could have been a distinctive dueling wound: a badge of honor. On his pudgy cheek, it signaled mere clumsiness. This man did not look as if he had ever been in a duel. His face glistened while his stubby pink hands were occupied. In one hand was a pocketknife with a Mother of Pearl handle; in the other was an uncut plug of chewing tobacco.

She introduced herself curtly but civilly. Then she plunked down the telegram concerning Liam's desertion. The first and only telegram ever to arrive at her family farm. The one-line message that jarred the entire McBurnie clan to the core. Without removing the tobacco or the knife, he nudged the document towards him and read it, looked up at her with a rather curious expression, and with the knife still in hand, he picked up his reading spectacles and read again. He took his time. She wondered why, as the message was only one line.

"*You said you was from Portland, Maine. This here is addressed to Cumberland County, Nova Scotia. That ain't around here.*"

She explained the telegram had been sent to her mother. The soldier in question was her brother, and they were extremely worried about him.

"*You should be,*" the Lieutenant grunted, giving her a sorrowful look. "*If we catch him, we'll court martial him. If found guilty, he could be shot. That's what we do with deserters if we ever caught any. If the rebels catch him, he'll wish we had caught him.*"

He pushed the telegram back at her.

"*Anyway,*" he sighed, "*he's long gone. They don't hang around once they make a break for it. They get as far away as they can get.*"

"*Could I see his military record? It might tell me something.*"

"*It won't tell you nothin', it ain't a fountain of information, your brother disappeared. Good Lord,*" he paused and looked sharply at her, "*he's been missing more than a year.*"

"*It took us a while to get organized,*" she said.

After her mother had given up hectoring everyone of influence in Nova Scotia, she started on the army of the United States, the Secretary of Defense, then General Grant, then Mr. Abraham Lincoln. When she failed to get a response, she began her campaign in earnest on her eldest daughter.

Meredith suddenly felt foolish and angry too. Angry at herself for being in this situation. Angry at her mother for her frenzied insistence. Angry at her suspicious fear that her mother, in such a hysterical state, might do the unthinkable and send one of her younger siblings. Jacob likely, but he had never been off the farm. Certainly not dour Janet or poor deranged Sarah. Dear God! They are babies.

After a long reflection, the Lieutenant was talking again. There was still no chaw in his mouth. In fact, she noticed he had put down the tobacco as if suddenly the need to chew wasn't important. Was it her that had changed his mind? He leaned back in his chair and folded his hands across his girth.

"*You say you're from Portland, I'm from Bath myself, you been there?*"

She lied and said she had, not wanting to show him what a new resident of Maine or even the United States, she really was.

He rambled on rather aimlessly, "*My father used to go to Portland a lot. He was a freight driver. Where's your husband?*"

The question was quick, without warning. It caught her off guard, trying as she was to keep her wits about her. She stared at him but didn't answer. She would, if possible, give him little personal information. He waited for her reply. The humid silence was only broken by a bluebottle softly buzzing at the window and the scuffing of the nervous foot of the private who had escorted her from the dock and had taken up guard duty against the far wall.

The Lieutenant reddened, his plump cheeks in full flush.

"*Maybe you haven't got a husband.*" He let loose a deep chuckle as if he had said something amusing. His face couldn't hide his disappointment when she did not respond. He wiped his brow and folded his hands again. "*Any children?*"

He was not a bad man she reasoned. Just a man spending time with her because he was bored with everything the army had to offer. She looked at him and smiled sweetly.

"*Nine,*" she said flatly, and this time the lanky soldier chuckled.

She thought she knew the Lieutenant at that moment, absorbing another slight, this one from a young, uppity woman. Maybe not the first time for that either.

He looked off in the distance, then down to his desk at the plug of tobacco.

"*When my dad hauled freight sometimes, I'd go along with him.*"

He smiled, and their eyes met, and she smiled back at him.

"*Half a dozen of our deserters got caught together up in the stump woods in Tennessee. Weren't the irregulars that caught them nor Hood's army, but our boys and the General wouldn't let them be shot as some claimed they were lost and not deserters. They sent them down to Nashville to muster them back in the army. We got Nashville and most of Tennessee under tight control. The city is under Military law now.*"

"*Nashville?*"

"*That's what they say, in Tennessee.*"

"*How far?*"

"*You can't go there. That's where the war is right now. The Confederates is up there under General Hood. They smashed us up pretty good in Corinth, but I bet this is gonna be the last hurrah for them rebels. It just gotta just drag on and on, don't it?*"

"*Tell me about Tennessee and how I get to Nashville.*"

He would not do that, he said. He got up then and walked around his desk and seemed to notice the young soldier for the first time.

"*Billy, ya don't have to be here. Can ya get us some coffee.*"

The young soldier left and returned with something the army called coffee, but it was the most vile tasting substance Meredith had ever experienced. It was army coffee, he explained sometimes the grounds have to be used more than once. For an instant, she wondered if they were playing some game with her, just to while away their time. Were they trying to poison her? She put the tin mug down and persisted on the question of Tennessee. Eventually, she saw her very first intuition about the Lieutenant to be correct. He couldn't hide his feelings. He wanted the war to be over so he could go home to Maine. He was as good a man as she had suspected. A family man with a wife he loved and five children, all daughters, he worried out loud about. This big slow-talking man cared not two fiddlesticks about the damn war. Listening to him drone on, Meredith wasn't certain if he even cared which side won. Traitorous maybe, but he desired conclusion more than victory. *"Except for the prisoners, the war is kind of over for us. I just want to go home."*

His name was Varley Thompson. To be precise, Lieutenant Second class Varley Leroy Thompson, a merchant by trade and a man, she sensed, who belonged in the army about as much as her brother.

He was hazy on details; never quite certain what trains were running and what tracks were blown up and not yet put right. Train times were a mystery. There was a spur line west, but the rebels had blown up the tracks. *"We patch em', they blow 'em up, and we do the same to their trains. Crazy ain't' it?"*

He paused frequently as if in deep thought, slowly scratching his chin. His features had a comical nature about them. Meredith thought he could be on the stage in some burlesque pantomime.

"If you go to Nashville you got to go with a lot of other people. You can't go traipsing through the woods around here, and the army can countermand a train leaving you high and dry. Besides, there ain't no train to Nashville right now, but there might be something: a way to get there, but if you could do it, it will be a hard trip. Take a while. The Presbyterian church people in Culpepper is organizing a wagon train to help the war refugees who have lost their homes. They say more than two dozen wagons is making their way to Nashville and on west from there. That's the safest way to travel, in the company of a lot of people. But whether they'd take you or have room for you, I don't know. A single woman, I don't know. It would be rough travel. You're doing something very dangerous young lady."

He showed what she thought was genuine concern, and it rather comforted her, made her feel less alone. The trepidation that had been building since her mother's letters increased in their desperation, somewhat eased in Meredith. The lessening of tension was due to the kernel of concern the Lieutenant had for her. His words gave her a little buoyancy as she could see the care in his eyes. He wasn't just saying the words. No con man or trickster could mimic the tenderness in this man's eyes. He was all thumbs, clumsy as an ox, and Meredith suspected his wife must love him dearly.

He was making a list for her with the young private helping. They had their heads bent over the desk, looking at a map as they debated the merits on routes if she decided to continue with the next leg of her journey, which apparently was into Tennessee. The Lieutenant was making her personal safety a priority. Even sending the soldier immediately out to learn what he could about what was moving west, when, and where.

"It gives Billy something to do," he confided. *"He really ain't in the army no more, ya know."*

She didn't know. The man was in uniform. How strange.

She left with Billy showing her the way to a large rooming house the Lieutenant had recommended. They were almost there, walking along a dusty street when a door was suddenly flung open, and Edward Foley was thrown down a set of steps into the street. His nose was bloody, and he had lost his hat, and if the three men beating him were any example of thoughtfulness and courtesy, it was doubtful it would be returned. They paid no attention to Meredith and her pleas for them to stop. She tried to intervene and assist the young lawyer, but Billy pulled her back. Finally, after kicking the nearly unconscious Foley, one of the attackers picked him up and threw him down a sharp embankment to a watery gully below.

"*We must help him,*" Meredith cried as one of the men turned to give her an ugly glare before walking away. Meredith started down the steep incline to the gully, but Billy took her arm again and hauled her back.

"*Leave, let him be.*"

"*Mr. Foley, are you alright?*" She called anxiously.

Foley, dazed and bloody, was picking himself up out of the shallow water. Billy pulled her up out of the embankment.

"*It is their fight,*" he said. "*Stupid confederates ain't nothin' to us.*"

"*But that man was on the riverboat with me. He is a lawyer. Why are they attacking him?*"

"They punch the daylights out of that sort. He's a peace preacher, those hereabouts who want the south to quit, to surrender. Them men who beat him might be deserters from Lee's army or veterans, who knows. They is all around us like nits on cow dung. There are people in the Confederacy ready to keep this here war going until they is all dead, every last one of them."

"So, you let the people you occupy beat each other and kill each other, and you do not raise a hand?"

Billy looked at her in a sympathetic manner. *"The more they kill each other, the less there is to fight."*

Suddenly the man Meredith had seen with Foley on the dock came out of the same building where she had first seen the attackers. His nose was bloody, and his shirt and jacket were ripped. He immediately went down the gully and assisted the lawyer.

"Sir, are you badly hurt?"

It was rather a silly question, but Foley was able to walk although bloody. His face was already swelling around the eyes and mouth.

"Thank you. Yes, it is the price we pay for urging peace in places peace is not wanted. There are those who will not see."

With the assistance of his colleague, Foley reached the top of the embankment.

"Thank you for your concern, Miss McBurnie. I have been attacked before, and no doubt will be again. It is the price we pay for a principle. If we can help bring this war to a speedier end and save one life, our reward will be in heaven.

He bowed to her. *"Enjoy your visit with your aunt."*

As the two men hobbled away, Billy said, *"So you a Miss, not married at all? What's he mean about an aunt. You got relatives here?"*

"No, he is mistaken. I have nobody here."

"Well, you got somebody now." He stepped back and saluted her.

"Private William Hunter at your service."

At that moment, Mr. and Mrs. Taylor drove by in a carriage. They did not notice her. Meredith reasoned they were on their way to nearby Fredericksburg. He appeared very grim, and she was pale and crying. Whatever relatives or friends had told the couple about their home had provided no comfort.

The boarding house recommended by the Lieutenant was a dump. There were rules posted everywhere – do not do this, do not do that. Even the water was rationed. The bedsheets were soiled, and so were most of the lodgers. Old stubble-chinned men, their feet unsteady, always about to lean into her in the dark hallways. There was not a lantern to be seen. Due to the amount of drunkenness and fornication, the rules meant nothing, and the unhealthy odor of the place was very disagreeable. An overbearing Scottish hen had charge of the kitchen or acted as if she did, taking a kettle of hot water right out of Meredith's hands and telling her she would have to wait.

"You're not the only one here, you know." Her brogue thick with a highland lilt heaped with sarcasm. They clashed later when Meredith waited for dinner at the large dining room table. The bossy woman managed to fork out the last pork chop for herself. It was too much.

In the morning, she returned to see if the Lieutenant had discovered any information concerning travel and informed him she was moving into the town's hotel. Lieutenant Thompson apologized if he had given her faulty information.

"Lieutenant, have you ever resided, say for just a night at the Coppersmith's Bed & Meal?"

He confessed he hadn't spent a night or even darkened the door of the establishment.

"Well, sir, without being presumptuous," which she knew she was, *"who gave you such a glowing recommendation?"*

He looked at her with such tragedy; the grief came off his face as a vapor that filled his office with steam-bath humidity. She had been playful, half-joking with him. They were becoming friends. Meredith genuinely liked him but realized her question had touched a still festering grief.

"They all dead now."

Meredith was stunned, *"I apologize Lieutenant Thompson, I did not mean, I was just being playful that's all. I am so sorry."*

"No," he waved away her apology as unnecessary. *"In war, people die. You did not start this war, and I did not start this war, but we are in it."*

They finally left the stuffy cabin and its sweltering heat for the slightly less dreadful heat outside. He wanted to talk about his family and what his home was like.

Meredith realized she was taking up a great deal of his day. Over her objections, Billy was dispatched to carry her luggage from the boarding house to the little hotel where she encamped. Thus, began an unusual comradeship between Meredith, Lieutenant Thompson, and Billy Hunter, the young private, who wore the blue uniform of the Union Army but was not really in the army.

"*You sure travel light,*" Billy said, almost disappointed there wasn't much for him to carry.

"*I did not have much to bring. Most of my possessions are in Maine. It is my plan to return to Portland and resume my work when my quest is complete*d."

"*I sure like the way you talk. Them words you speak sure sounds nice.*"

Later in the day, Billy told the Lieutenant, "*She's got a nice room.*" Proud to have been, however briefly, in her hotel room.

Looking back, Meredith would remember her days in Falmouth as a rather wistful and highly unusual time in her life. The three of them would sit in the dining room of her run-down hotel, sipping sherry as if they were old comrades in arms. Two bored men: a Christian merchant from Bath, Maine longing for his family, a discharged private soldier, who tried to hide his distinct southern drawl, and a tall, straight young woman, mature for her age but still a child in many ways. She had never before tasted sherry.

Taking their time about it as if they lingered on purpose, enjoying each others' company while narrowing the list of options. The sister of a deserter was receiving first-class treatment from the United States Army. It was nothing he wouldn't do for his own daughters, the Lieutenant told her, blushing with eyes full of feeling.

She already knew things about Private Hunter but didn't understand why he was still wearing his uniform. It was becoming obvious he was sweet on her, and try as he might, he could never quite conceal it. Even the Lieutenant wore a broad smile as Billy Hunter offered again to guide Meredith wherever she needed to go.

There were many curious aspects to Private William S. Hunter. He seemed to be permanently attached to the Lieutenant with no real responsibilities. The Lieutenant called him Billy, not Private, and treated him as a friend rather than an underling.

It took a few days for Meredith to begin to understand things. War is seldom what it seems. It had come and gone, and they just wanted it to be done with so much in fact that they ignored the reality of things. Blood was being spilled in another part of Virginia, in a place called Walthall Junction, where armies were engaged in a fierce battle that very day. The serenity of this tiny bubble of Falmouth was just a delusion. The war was all around them, but just far enough away not to hear the cannon fire. Meredith penned a report to the Clarks' and a letter to her parents, informing them she had arrived and had made contact with the army. Contact was such a funny word for it. She reported to the Lieutenant's office every morning, walking through the space where a sea of empty tents had sat for many months but was suddenly gone. Only their imprint on the ground told the story. Her mission in the morning was to see if there was any news on prisoners of war in Tennessee or any avenue of travel to Nashville. Then they would meet in the afternoon for sherry. The Lieutenant didn't seem to have much to do when there were no prisoners in the camp.

Still, Meredith eventually realized how the war had scarred these two men. They had seen all its chaotic circumstances and deadly gore. It became more apparent when Billy got a wagon and took her down the road to Fredericksburg: the first city mauled by this war between north and south, often between families and brothers. Close to twenty thousand men had perished or disappeared there.

Although it had been an ultimate Confederate victory, the Union Army initially had deeply scarred the community. For a brief time, the federal army held Fredericksburg. Federal cannons blew fine houses to splinters, sending the crazed citizenry, men, women, and children, running for their lives.

Billy was pointing out the streets where he had fought.

"*I set some of them houses on fire myself. Never thought as a soldier I'd be settin' fires. I can see them womenfolk and children running. It was December; it snowed the night before when we let the cannon rip. Some of them folks was half-dressed, the kids bawling, runnin' in their bare feet, houses burning. It wasn't what I thought the war would be: making babies cry.*"

Meredith listened and looked and wondered where the Taylor's house was located. She asked herself if she would stop and talk to them. What would she say? Commiserate on their property destruction and the vile state of the war. Would they even be interested in talking to her? She would be seen as a Yankee. Mr. and Mrs. Taylor did not like Yankees. Just as well, they were nowhere in sight.

"*Never thought a soldier be settin' fires,*" Billy repeated. "*I was hurt here.*"

When it took her another day to realize what that word "hurt" meant, Meredith, cursed herself for being so terribly unperceptive. How could she ever find the nuances of a story, the little things that bring an article alive when she was so unobservant? "Hurt," in Billy Hunter's case, was having his entire left foot blown off by a cannonball.

Meredith shuddered at her lack of awareness. They had been together for a few days, and she failed to notice his left foot was a block of wood, skillfully carved and molded to resemble a foot. It was painted black and did look like a boot. Nonetheless, Meredith told herself, she should have noticed. It explained the slight hitch in Billy's walk. It didn't explain why she had walked by his side several times but never once looked at his feet.

Billy was everywhere, waiting in the hotel lobby in the mornings to escort her wherever she wished to go. They visited the Lieutenant first to hear if there was any news on the wagon train for war immigrants. Then they would take a morning stroll, walking side by side chatting about her upcoming journey. Meredith finally noticed his foot when they came to a raised wooden sidewalk where they had to step up. Billy had a little trouble with it. He had to turn sideways and place one foot securely on the step and lift the other foot. When she finally noticed his wooden foot, Meredith gaped like a child observing its first reptile, believing and not believing what was before her. He quickly steadied her.

"*When people say I'm not all there, well, they are right.*" He laughingly declared, trying to lessen her shock. They walked along a road that bordered the river.

"*A carpenter in our unit fashioned my foot. My stump goes into it, and I hold it on with leather straps around my knee. Not too bad ah; and no toenails to look after.*"

They went on in silence for several minutes until they came down to a tranquil place where a fallen tree trunk provided a place to sit and watch the slow passing waters of the Rappahannock. Billy continued,

"So that's why I'm not in the army anymore. The Lieutenant lets me hang around until I'm all healed. But the general is coming back to camp with the whole army soon, and I'll have to scat."

"But you could go home." Meredith said, *"there is nothing stopping you."*

Billy demurred, hummed, and hawed a bit, played the part of some good old country boy, all quaintness one moment and the manners of a rural gentleman the next. She made him stop his foolishness, and he finally agreed he would soon go somewhere but probably not home. His medical discharge had arrived. He guessed he was ready to go.

"Then why are you still here?"

Meredith pulled it out of him. It was partly what Lewis Clark, her editor in Portland, called the natural journalist in her. She was driven to uncover things, naively believing the truth would set everyone free. She would dig and dig because she could not stop herself. Eventually, she was sure she would discover his secrets, the inner workings of this young man. But with ex-Private William Hunter, she would do it gently.

Billy was green around girls, and Meredith, with childish delusion, believed herself to be a skilled interviewer. Maybe she was, or maybe Billy's crush on her was enough. It didn't take long before he was telling her everything, and she finally understood.

He came from Hendersonville, deep down on the Mississippi. That was a start, she thought and waited for more. A little prompting at just the right time and this ex-soldier with the wooden foot told her everything and in the manner of a skilled storyteller. She could imagine him as a boy, sitting on the floor by the cracker barrel in a country store listening to the old men spinning their tall tales of the Mexican Wars and other things. Stories embellished with each passing decade as verification of the truth became less likely or important.

When Billy opened up and really started talking about his life, he somehow became a changed person. He had just turned twenty, two years older than Meredith, but he suddenly sounded as if he had lived a lifetime. He could not read or write and never had a chance for schooling. Chores at home and out working like a man at the age of fourteen. A carpenter's apprentice for his father, and if he measured wrong and ruined a piece of lumber, he would get a licking with that very piece of wood. Except he said, within the hour or two, that ruined piece of lumber would find a use.

He was doing all right he told her. He had met a wonderful girl who could write her name, and they were going to marry. Then Scarlet fever carried her off, and a heartbroken Billy joined the army. There was more of course, the darker side that didn't come as easily. He hesitated, pulled back, but Meredith coached him along, and she got it out of him. He was a soldier who would rather take his rifle and blow out his brains than cry in front of her. But Billy Hunter, close to tears, admitted the rest of it. He was alone in the world and felt the emptiness of it. His father, an avowed abolitionist, had died with John Brown. His mother, her nerves rubbed raw, was in a lunatic institution. Billy thought he had plenty of brothers and sisters, he knew some of them, by different mothers because Daddy was a lady's man and got around a bit. He did not know how many siblings for certain.

"I'll get no work back home."

"But you don't know that Billy."

That most tragic expression told her what should have been obvious. He came from a Confederate state and had served in the Union army. There would be no going home for Billy Hunter.

"I would always be the traitor with the wooden foot. I can look ahead and see my life. I'll always be poor, and if I lived to be a feeble old man, the youngsters would throw green apples at me and call me names. I'd always be the traitor."

He leaned forward and caved into Meredith, wrapping his arms around her in a mad embrace. She didn't know what else to do but to hold him. There were no words to answer him, to tell him things would be all right because those were feeble words and hollow words and very likely untrue words. Meredith felt him tremble in his strong embrace as ripples of despair and longing ran up and down his spine. When he finally released her, they were both dizzy and out of breath.

"Come with me," she said without hesitation or consideration. The invitation was purely out of sympathy. She seldom acted or spoke in the spur of the moment, but the words were spoken coming out of their embrace. *"You're out of the army. You could accompany and assist me and end up somewhere else; Tennessee or California maybe where you could start over."*

He didn't speak but tightly embraced her again.

"*Of course,*" she said, loosening his grasp, "*we would have to have some ground rules.*" Straightening up, she held his shoulders. "*I'm leaving right away. If you decide to join me, it looks like our best chance is with the refugees.*"

Chapter 4

The lieutenant was delighted. He thanked Meredith that evening when Billy had left the table for more sherry. *"No one cared at first if Billy hung around and still wore his uniform, the captain was getting impatient, but he let it be as he had other matters to worry about. But the general and troops are coming back to camp. He'll order me to tell Billy to clear out. I'm glad I don't have to do that."*

"He hasn't actually informed me he would accompany me," Meredith replied.

"Oh, he is going with you all right. He's just not particular over that list of rules. He don't care for the fact you two will be colleagues and associates only. He wanted to pretend you were romantically connected."

"I am not here for romance. I fear I may have led him on already, although that was not my intention. I do not want him getting any ideas."

The lieutenant chuckled. *"He's got ideas already. He's besotted."*

"You are very close to Billy, aren't you?"

"I was there when his foot got shot off. A five-pounder made a bloody rainbow when it hit him, scattering Billy's toes into the atmosphere, his foot flying in a thousand pieces. Billy was not a target; he was just in the way. That cannonball had another mission. It crashed into a platoon of soldiers. Billy was luckier than them, but he truly suffered and almost bled to death. We was quartermasters, assigned to the New York regiment cause all their people were dead. Things get mixed up in wartime. We should not have been there, but Billy and me got called up when the generals decided we were attacking Fredericksburg. I put the tourniquet on Billy's leg myself; two tourniquets actually, cause I wasn't certain where the first one should go. My heart was pounding that day. Too much," he smiled at her weakly while mopping his brow, *"it was too much to see."* He

wanted to say more, something personal. Billy had been gone longer than usual. Was this planned, Meredith wondered.

Lieutenant Varley Thompson was in uniform. He had removed his hat when they entered the hotel dining room. It was humid, his hair was sticking to his forehead. Looking down at the bare table, he began again.

"*We did things in the war I didn't like, things I am ashamed of. Things I wouldn't want my children to know, so I don't know why I am telling you,*" he chuckled uncomfortably, "*but Billy did things, and he lives with it too, knowin' what he done.*"

"*Tell me.*"

"*I have no right to tell you. They were shameless acts we done. No need for it. You see we was camped in town, right smack dab in the center of Fredericksburg. We'd taken the town early on, and we was camped in the midst of the enemy, and us soldiers were left alone to make our own way. First, the boys went looking for liquor. Well turns out a merchant had a cellar full of hard cider, and that fueled the ransacking of houses looking for more liquor and anything else that could be stolen. Myself I ransacked a few looking for food, but the boys were breaking stuff and looting things right in front of the homeowners. I drank stolen liquor that night, entered houses that weren't mine, and took stuff that wasn't mine. But,*" he gave a giant sigh, "*I gave it back.*"

"*You gave it back?*"

"*Yes, who knows, in ordinary times, they might be nice people, but that woman was not nice to me. She hissed at me like a snake, called me filthy Yankee trash, with me standing there, in her doorway, with both my arms wrapped around her mantle clock that I had removed the night before.*"

He paused and looked directly at Meredith. "*I guess I need to tell somebody.*" Saying that, he sat back in his chair. "*See, I am not as nice a person as you may have thought.*"

He mopped his brow, "*You see, when we got there, we wasn't fighting the confederate army. They weren't even there yet. When the rebels did arrive, we lost many men, but at first, we was fighting civilians, not fighting really, just tormenting them, scaring the devil out of them. Those kids.*" He looked away, and she saw something in his eyes that looked like tears welling up. "*I hate war.*" He said. "*I would not want my children to be treated that way.*"

Before more was said, Billy returned with refilled glasses, and there was no more talk of Fredericksburg. A much better idea was a series of farewell toasts: the final decision having been made. Meredith would try to hitch a place on one of the refugee wagons. Once more, the lieutenant and Billy felt it would be irresponsible not to speak of the slim chance of her success in finding her brother. How could it be otherwise? Where would she look? Then Billy boldly informed her, despite the absolute absurdity of her mission, he would escort her. Overcome with emotion, Meredith kissed him tenderly on the cheek and immediately wished she hadn't. The lieutenant watched them with a faint smile that Meredith knew was forced. He was losing two friends. Maybe the only friends he had in the army. Maybe all his army buddies were already dead. Meredith suspected the lieutenant was greatly missing his wife and daughters. He looked very subdued amid cheerful toasts.

The following day, with tears in her own eyes, Meredith put her arms around the lieutenant's great girth and embraced him tenderly. He had been such a gift to her; an unexpected and much-appreciated gift. She embarrassed him with her words of gratitude. They said their good-byes and Billy smartly saluted before they boarded a freight barge to take them upriver to catch the branch line for the thirty-mile trip to Culpepper.

It was a gamble. There might not be room. The Presbyterians might say no. The wagon train was for refugees displaced by the war, not for a frantic foreigner looking for a deserter. However, Meredith had a very official looking letter from the United States Army, identifying her as a non-combatant, a native of Nova Scotia, a colony of the British crown and giving her the right to pass through enemy lines. Meredith cautioned Billy to refrain from mentioning desertion. They would take a chance. The wagons were heading south and then west to Nashville and beyond into the Great Plains.

Thousands had lost everything. The homeless were making their escape in great waves across the continent. Leaving one danger for another. They were avoiding the war but facing the threat of hostile Indians or worse, cutthroat irregulars and militias roaming the Missouri borderlands. The woods were filled with lost and hungry deserters from both armies. There were many stories, mostly made-up, but some had a ring of truth. They said Union and Confederate deserters had run into each other in some swamp water wilderness, and even though they had run away from the war, somehow the fight was still in them. They had their own mini civil war in that swamp. The battle lasted seven minutes, and when both sides were out of ammunition, they declined to participate in hand-to-hand combat with bayonets and knives. After all, they were deserters. The former slaves who had joined the U.S. Army at least had grub and clothing, but other slaves had just run, as far and as fast as possible. They were in the wilderness along with cutthroats, displaced farm families, and camp followers from both armies who had tarried too long and lost their way. A wagon train might also face natural calamities, storms, floods, or wild animals in the many miles ahead.

"Come back if it's no good," the lieutenant told her, "don't go striking out on your own."

On the train, Meredith saw the Scottish vixen from the smelly boarding house. The one who had taken the last pork chop was preoccupied scribbling in a notebook. I suppose, Meredith thought, she will keep popping up like a reoccurring ailment.

At dawn the next morning, fifty-six wagons circled the yard in front of a little white wooden Presbyterian church in Culpepper, Virginia. From their canvas tops came the cries of wailing infants and barking dogs, accompanying the bumping and braying of horses. There was singing and praying and profanity too in a thick Irish brogue. Meredith heard many languages and heated discussions and disagreements, what sounded like insults hurled in guttural dialects of Germanic Dutch. More church people arrived with last-minute supplies rounded up locally from people who placed Christian charity above Yankee hatred. The aroma of breakfast biscuits, coffee, and frying bacon blended with axle grease and steaming horse feces. The church ladies had put on a wonderful bon voyage for the travelers. The canvas tops were tightened while casks and trunks that could not be fitted inside the wagon box were lashed to the outsides and the knots checked twice. Harnessing was inspected. A few horses were nervous, pulling at their harness, their hooves frantically stamping the ground. Old hunting dogs ran back and forth, excited by the medley of much labor and many voices.

Going from one wagon to another were two distinct couples. Meredith issued a sigh as she again noticed the pork chop thief standing next to a slightly stooped, round-shouldered little man. This time the Scottish woman, whose name was Pauline McKendrick, saw Meredith too and remembered her from somewhere. How tall and straight she stood next to the spindly young fellow who was having trouble with his hands. He had thrust them into each pocket of his new coat and trousers, seeing if he could find a proper fit for them. Inside his breast pocket, neatly folded by her own hand, were Meredith's ground rules. Billy Hunter had shed his uniform.

Chapter 5

Pauline McKendrick was as anxious as anyone to secure a place on the wagon train. When Meredith spotted her on the train to Culpepper, Pauline had been writing in her diary. She and her husband also had to wait several days in Falmouth, and they saw their only avenue to Nashville was to take a chance with the refugees. That very morning, she had written-

"Tell me what can ruin a life more thoroughly than war. Even if it doesn't dip you in blood or tear from you, those you love, it can still provide a most challenging inconvenience. Your well-ordered life, suddenly gone in one night, in one fire. Everything lost. Even the precious wee things brought from Edinburgh."

She had done her best, she supposed. Certainly, she could have married better. The old thing was faithful like an aging dog. Honestly, she told herself, her Isaac was beginning to look like an old dog too. Wrinkles around those hound-like eyes that she could never refuse. Not wrinkles but bags really, making him appear even more droopy. He always looked like an unmade bed anyway. Some men wear their clothes with such flare as if the garment was part of them. Her husband wasn't one of those men.

She had long since given up attempts at reforming or even scolding. The man would nod and do nothing. Besides, the old thing was happy. She would keep him because once, every so often, he would come up with a really clever idea. Where that intelligence came from, she could never determine. His good ideas rose to the surface after dislodging from some hidden cavern in his cortex. She could have married a doctor.

If not properly schooled herself, at least she had a taste of higher education. Uncle Ned had seen to all that and seen to her too. When she was sixteen and beginning to bloom in a most attractive manner, he had just returned from India, smelling of brandy and handing out presents as if it was Saint Nicholas himself. Within a fortnight, he took her aside and declared he could not keep his hands off her. He was right about that, and her diary might just as well know about it because everybody else did. Ned was never a man to keep his hands to himself. It got him killed too, but before that, Pauline had experienced a privately tutored small class for young ladies. She had a taste at least of Greek and Latin before Uncle Ned was shot. She had two years and a bit of that very wonderful life before they came with that dreadful news of Uncle Ned's demise. Pauline confided much to her diary, including that the cost of her education was Uncle Ned thrusting himself upon her. She was young and foolish enough to be flattered. She let him look at things and touch things. She pleased him by stroking his johnny. She pulled away very suddenly if he tried to remove her clothing. One June night, outside, in the woods, she let him take her. School was worth it, every bit of it. She would, she often told herself, do it again without hesitation.

Her relationship with her mother was caustic. They had never gotten along. Her mother was a tramp, and Uncle Ned couldn't keep his hands off her mother either. Yes, she knew Uncle Ned was not, "really" her, "Uncle," but it was simply more convenient "with him living with us," Pauline at seventeen was told by her tipsy mother.

Uncle Ned died quickly, felled by a bullet from a homesteader whose wife was highly insulted by having her bottom massaged by an experienced but uninvited hand. Things quickly fell apart for Pauline. There was no money for school, and Ma had completely taken to the bottle. Besides herself, there were four hungry bellies to fill. It took her three years of grinding poverty before the oldest ones went into service or apprenticeship. She sold herself a few times when they were starving. She moved to Edinburgh and acquired a position as a kitchen maid to a kind couple near Holyrood Castle, a very good neighborhood with less likelihood of hooligans around to torment her. A woman walking alone could never be too careful. The job gave her a lifeline.

Saving enough, she booked steerage for three, taking her two younger sisters with her. They were twelve and nine. Neither survived the voyage. Some contagion went through the ship after twenty days at sea. Thirty-nine days out, and a third of the passengers were dead.

That was the experience of the lady waiting for the wagon train with her husband at the Presbyterian church in Culpepper, Virginia. Pauline McKendrick was then wanting and waiting for that new chapter in her life.

Although they were not aware of it, Pauline McKendrick and Meredith McBurnie had one thing in common early on. Neither of them liked the wagon master. Dwight Chandler was busy and gruff and wore his gruffness on his stiff weathered face. Only his drooping white mustache softened his appearance so that high on his horse, he resembled a great unwelcome warrior. He was not a gentleman at all and cared not a whit about those wanting to hitch a ride.

"*Space is scarce,*" was his only comment. Meredith and Billy went from one wagon to another. Some people hardly spoke English and did not understand her as Meredith was doing all the talking. The wounded veteran at her side was standing at attention, appearing wooden and ill at ease.

It was a good thing she was conducting the conversation. Meredith was convincing; a maiden in distress, only a cad, could refuse assistance. She returned to the wagon master giving him such an endearing smile of helplessness. Billy thought the entire universe had just opened up. How beautiful she was. He would carry her off to Nashville on his shoulders if he had to. Yet she never smiled at him the way she was smiling at this overstuffed guy with the big mustache.

Although Billy was much moved by her pleadings, Chandler was not.

"*You might try the potter,*" one of the women told her, "*he mentioned he would like a hand with the reins.*" Ten minutes later, Meredith and Billy were looking up at a plump little man in a derby hat with a short stubby beard. His hair, slightly graying at the temples, gave him a distinguished air of respectability. That appearance was further enhanced by his reading spectacles.

"*I'd like some assistance with the driving, but I require an experienced driver or ex-soldier or an out-of-work drover if there is such a thing these days. Besides, there is only room for one, which means it would have to be this here fella, young lady.*" For the first time, he looked directly at Billy.

"*Got your own grub?*"

"Yes," Meredith replied. "*We both have beans, salt pork, dried beef, and porridge and bedrolls too.*" The Lieutenant had rooted around for any army supplies he could find, telling her to take the additional blanket he was offering.

The potter rubbed his chin. "*It's cramped, but for a dollar a week, I can fit one in.*"

"*My brother can ride up with you. I don't take up any space.*" She exclaimed before Billy could get a word out of his mouth. "*He can handle the horses too. If you want to rest a spell, I'll move upfront with him.*"

Billy stared at her in alarm, fascination and admiration mixed in an emotional concoction he could not identify. It bothered him that Meredith called him her brother. Her ground rules were bad enough, but he understood she must protect her reputation and chastity. He would be a gentleman because that's how to win a lady's hand. If he survived, that is, because Billy Hunter felt he might swoon and die at her feet that very moment.

"*That would be a dollar a week each,*" said the potter. "*Two dollars,*" declared Meredith. "*Surely you wouldn't charge a slender woman like me the same as a hefty man.*"

The potter squinted; he couldn't distinguish much difference between the two of them. The young man was skin and bones, but he thought it would be nice to have someone for company as comely as the young woman.

"*Alright, dollar and a half a week for both of you, but you do the cookin'.*"

Meredith nodded, and the potter rose and reached down from his wagon, holding out his hand to seal the deal.

Ninety minutes later, as church members completed passing out baskets of home cooking for the travelers and the last of the well-wishes were delivered, and the final prayers went up to God, the wagon master called everyone together. They stopped what they were doing, and the people gathered around him. Chandler stood with his arms on his hips and waited for quiet. He was a tower of a man, well over six feet in height with a barrel chest and broad shoulders. His two big wolfhounds sat in front of him. His outriders, Tim and Ned, flanked the wagon master. The people stopped talking, and the buzz of the crowd went silent. Even the two dozen children understood that the gathering was somehow important.

"*Now listen to me.*" Chandler's voice was strong and clear. "*I hope you people have not been misinformed. We are beginning a dangerous trek. The woods and wilderness you will be traveling through are filled with wild Indians, outlaw militias, run-away slaves, and deserters from both armies. Some of those people will be hungry, some of em' will be starved, and they will be desperate. I have discovered that desperate people will do anything. They will kill for food. Some of these militias have full bellies, but they lust for blood. They hate Yankees. They consider themselves patriots, but what they really are is cutthroats. We are going through this country during war, and some of you come from the north and some from the south. But on this wagon train.*"

He paused and looked around him.

"*Beginning right now, you are not rebel nor Yankee. While you are under my care, there is no war. You will not take sides, and you will not talk about sides. You will not talk about the war at all. Anyone who does or who agitates or in any way or causes trouble will be made to go it alone.*"

He stopped again, letting the words sink in, taking his time to resume. The group had encircled him, and he turned to give every member a stern glare.

"*You do not want to go it alone. You are safer with numbers. With the wagon train, there is at least some safety. I have been doing this for a long time, in war and in peace. There are always one or two troublemakers who cannot conform and are kicked out to make it by themselves. Do you know anyone such as that?*"

He stopped again and waited. Then in a clear, cold voice, he snarled, "*Do you know anyone such as that?*" Stone silence. He continued. "*No, you do not because those people are dead. Scalped, knifed, shot, mutilated. Dead is dead. You will do as I say at all times. When I say move, you will move; when I say stay, you will stay. Tim and Ned are my outriders. Besides myself, they are the only ones giving orders here. Is that understood?*"

Silence. Not a question from the four hundred. Chandler clapped his hands once with great force. "*Good, then on your wagons, let us be on our way.*"

The outriders went down the trail. The potter gave the reins a shake and a brisk command to his horses, and they were moving. Their wagon was the fourth from the front. Meredith felt the first sway of the vehicle as it lurched into motion. A child was crying somewhere behind them. Pots tied to the wagon sides clanged, making an awful racket. Dogs excitedly barked, and the wheels of many wagons crunched on the gravel as they rolled out of the churchyard with parishioners waving their farewells. Meredith was sitting in the back, trying to adjust to the swaying and pitching. It was most uncomfortable. They passed a cemetery with many graves of the recently fallen. The community was behind them, but patchy farms dotted the landscape. They were on their way, and within an hour, the countryside was suddenly barren.

The potter's wagon was crammed with the tools of his trade: barrels of clay, tins of paint, and a large kiln that took up much of the wagon box, forcing Meredith to make a small nest for herself hard against the back brace. The wagon rocked back and forth continually. The motion made her ill. She had spent plenty of time on a hay wagon which was luxury compared with the jostling and swaying she was then experiencing. She soon learned the second blanket was a blessing as her bedroll became her cushion. It was often easier just to get out and walk, as many women and children were already doing.

The rules were strictly enforced. They could not stop for the night until they came to an open space where the wagons could be drawn in a circle. The outriders stopped at every wagon to tell them again, never wander away, never. Men would take turns on guard duty. As soon as they stopped for the night, those not on guard duty would gather whatever wood they could find for the fires. Those were Mr. Chandler's rules. He and one outrider would be ahead of them to scout the land and warn of danger. The second outrider would be behind the wagon train. Nobody would be sneaking up on them.

Their wagons rumbled on. The early excitement was already waning. It was almost dark when Mr. Chandler came back and announced it would be another hour before they could camp for the night and a great deal of grumbling began as the news went down the line in two or three different languages. So, Meredith's first meal on the trail for Billy and the potter was fixed by lantern light and a silvery moon overhead. She made biscuits, and they shared beans soaked since morning but still almost uneatable. Nobody complained. They were exhausted.

They would sleep under the stars or under the wagon if it was raining. Billy puts his bedroll as close as possible to Meredith. *"There's a lot of foreigners here,"* he whispered. Her ear had already caught strange languages the potter said were German and Gaelic.

"*Everybody lookin' for a better place to live,*" Billy said.

Not Meredith. She would be happy back in Portland, correcting copy and writing an occasional short piece that might or might not get in the magazine. How far she felt from that employment. How far she felt from everything.

The days started to repeat themselves; up at dawn, wash oneself quickly as best you could from a basin. Filling up the water kegs if a brook was handy. Mr. Chandler rationed everything, including water. If there was little water to wash with, they wiped away the dust and dirt with a dry cloth. Then long hours swaying back and forth in the rear of the potter's wagon or walking beside it, mile upon weary mile. Her legs ached, telling her it was time to climb back on board. Mr. Chandler said Nashville would take fifty-five days with good weather and no trouble.

"*What are you gonna do if ya can't find ya brother there,*" asked Billy one night.

"*Keep going, I guess,*" she replied.

"*Goin' where?*"

"*I think west or maybe south,*" she said. "*Keep going somewhere.*"

She would go all the way. Dash into the Pacific Ocean or the Gulf of Mexico if she had to and announce to her mother, she had crossed the entire continent and had not found him. She had done all she could do. Then she would go back to Portland and resume her work.

The potter's name was James McCarthy. He was a short, stout, genial enough man who had lost his wife the year before in the New England floods when a dam had collapsed. Billy drove at times, and Meredith made the meals. The three of them got along well enough, although Meredith had a growing concern over Billy. In Falmouth, her spontaneous decision to invite Billy to join her, while rash, at least at the time, seemed sensible. He was so lost. But now, whenever Billy saw her walking behind the wagon, he immediately jumped down to join her until McCarthy wanted a break from the reins.

The potter himself sometimes joined Meredith to stretch his legs. But the potter walking beside Meredith particularly bothered Billy. He would stand up with the reins in his hands, looking over the sides, trying to watch them. If McCarthy noticed, he didn't let on, but Meredith certainly noticed. Billy was becoming exceedingly jealous.

"*Watch what you're doing,*" yelled McCarthy once, when Billy was paying more attention to them than the horses and almost put the wagon off the rutted road.

In the third week, many of the travelers were becoming belligerent and short-tempered. Their nerves rubbed raw by the discomfort, the years of war with all its misery, regret left by the loss of property, and heartfelt grief over the loss of loved ones. There was growing resentment, too, particularly towards the immigrant families who spoke little English. One of them had done something to cause offense to a hard-bitten Irish farm couple with a flock of kids. Meredith could often hear bickering in the wagons down the line, but it was Billy that mostly troubled her. He was continually scowling and becoming antagonistic towards everyone: particularly potter McCarthy. Meredith firmly told Billy to stop it. "*He's done nothing to offend you.*"

Billy muttered under his breath. "*He's got his eye on you.*"

"*He doesn't. And what if he does? I'm not here for romance or to find a husband. I've explained all that to you already. Read the ground rules. You are my traveling companion, not my beau or betrothed.*"

"*I've got to look after you.*"

"*No, you don't. I can look after myself. Stop being nasty to Mr. McCarthy.*"

Without another word, Billy climbed back on the wagon. He remained pensive and quiet the following days as their caravan crept across the rolling hills, fields, tangled forests, and past empty farms and once prosperous villages.

Despite the hopelessness of her search, when given the opportunity, Meredith never lost the chance to make inquiries, to ask the same question. Yes, local people would respond. They had seen plenty of drifters, all right. Rag-tag men, deserters, still in their filthy uniforms, passing by in twos or threes. They would steal food if not offered any, but no, never a flaxen-haired flute player, who could earn his dinner by a tune or a quick sketch of a family member.

At the end of the third week, a fist fight broke out while the weary travelers were fixing food for the evening meal. It began with two men, and soon five or six brawlers were involved: punching and tussling on the ground. One man was thrown into a fire. The shrieks of his children matched his cry of distress. Chandler rode up and knocked two of the men on the head with his rifle butt.

"*Behave or get out, goddamn it,*" he barked, hauling in his horse to physically separate the warring parties. Things were never right in the wagon train after that initial fierce altercation. There was always tension between the Europeans and the Irish and those who thought themselves thoroughly American. Even on the move, when Chandler wasn't close by, there was heckling, and harsh comments tossed back and forth from one wagon to another. The Irish had a grudge against the Dutch or German immigrants. While some other immigrants clashed with each other, often answering in a language not understood except by its harsh tone. A young Irish family with a gaggle of kids hurled insults at the wagon next to them. The mother, who was a youngster herself, had kicked someone's dog. The dog's owner took offense. Two twelve-year-old boys got into a fight that led to their parents having hard words. Those little needling disputes occurred daily. Occasionally, there were smiles and even music some evenings, and once a youngster got his foot run over by a wagon wheel, and there was help and care offered. The women often walked in small groups by their wagons, talking of their families. Some of the women worried because their husbands wanted to break away and go off on their own. Danger kept them together.

Then suddenly, they were in a new type of territory with woods so deep and dark the branches formed a canopy above them that shut out most of the daylight. It was impossible to sit in the wagons on the corduroy roads but too dark to walk without stumbling, and snarly branches of thorns tore your clothing. Thickets of gnarled feathery pine and thorny brambles grew over the roads and trails. They were different from anything Meredith had seen in her native Nova Scotia. Everyone was warned again that the country was filled with deserters and desperate men. How ironic, Meredith thought. She was looking for a deserter, and the woods were full of them. Maybe she should adopt one and send him home to mother. It was only later she felt guilty for thinking such a thing. Chandler's outrider Tim said the war had driven some men mad. In hushed tones, the women talked of such things as madness. They all had their personal war experiences. Stories told that could tear the heart out of a person. Stories of lost homes and lost sons. The war had touched them all. Over the long miles, they discussed what they had read in the newspapers and penny press of

Confederate militias and blood-curdling stories of red Indians taking women prisoner. That's why the drivers carried their rifles next to them on the wagons. Meredith saw few remnants of war in the early days with the wagon train. But war in Virginia was impossible to avoid.

On a blistering hot morning, a sudden sharp miasma struck them as if the wagon train had crossed into hell itself. A wall of horrible odor stretched across the landscape. Soon they saw the cause of it. An open field, flattened grass, trees barren of branches, or once-stately limbs hanging in broken surrender. Some tree trunks had been shattered into splinters by cannon. A nearby ridge was dotted with fresh graves. The rough wooden crosses were so close they formed a fence. The soldiers had been buried but not the animals. The stink of rotting animal corpses was sickening. It offended the nostrils, and the residue of decay assaulted the eyes. Silently the wagons crept across the battlefield as birds, large and small, swooped in and out, and danced around the decay.

There was a curious silence from the caravan. It took a full hour to pass through the scene. The scavengers, both human and animals, had already plundered the wreckage. Steel, iron, anything blown to smithereens that could be salvaged was gone. Horse meat fit to eat was gone too. Grapeshot peppered the ground. It reminded Meredith of pebbles on the beach near her town. She surveyed the scene from the back of the wagon with no desire to set foot on grass stained with blood. They came upon vast weedy fields later that day where plows had once split the rich topsoil. The trail took them by empty farms where the slapping door of a pig pen was the only welcome. The wagon train came upon crowded hovels filled with sullen faces and hollow-eyed children. The passing armies, both north, and south had taken their livestock. No, they had never heard of Liam. Clusters of people were moving aimlessly across the countryside. Occasionally they came upon families of former slaves who looked lost in their newfound freedom. Wagons full of belongings moved in the opposite direction. A family on a farm horse. They wanted information concerning what was ahead of them. They had never heard of anyone called Liam.

Both official armies in blue and gray and the vigilantes and militias had grievously raped every part of the countryside. The people were victims for all sides to plunder. Even if the warring forces and cutthroats had not spilled blood, there was

always the constant search for food to feed their members. Both sides blew up railroads that could have delivered badly needed supplies to their own troops. The warehouses in Washington and Richmond were crammed full of medical bandages, ointments, cans of beef, barrels of flour, and hardtack. There the supplies sat, with no method
of delivery. Farm children in the warring states had been trained what to do when the far-off thunder of hoofbeats was heard. Chickens were to be grabbed by the feet, two at a time, and Johnny, you run like hell into the woods to where livestock was hidden. Every living thing was to be rushed into a predetermined place. Concealing food kept families from starving.

They all had stories along the way. Meredith heard many accusations that the Federal army was destroying all the crops in Virginia. At the first substantial town they pulled into, Meredith set about asking everyone in sight about Liam, his ability to draw, and his mastery of the flute. They mostly stared at her with blank expressions.

Meanwhile, the wagon train was shrinking. Seven of the wagons were leaving. The Dutch immigrants wanted to go off by themselves. Mr. Chandler told them they were obstinate fools. They were coming closer to the war and were safer in greater numbers. If they understood him, they were not convinced.

In ten more days, the canvas-topped train rolled into Kentucky. Mr. Chandler gathered them around him again following the evening meal. He reminded them all if stopped by Confederate irregulars, they were Virginians, from the counties around, Falmouth and Culpepper, faithful to the southern cause.

"There is a Confederate army ahead of us," he said. *"If they are well trained and disciplined there should be no trouble. If they are not, and they hear those Yankee vowels some of you are spouting, there could be trouble. It is wise to never forget that some of you are from the northern states and that you are in enemy territory. These people ahead of us are not the church folks who organized your caravan."*

Kentucky, a border state, had rolling hills and strange vegetation. Wildflowers and foxes poked out from the underbrush. The wagon families were constantly on edge, rifles at the ready. Down the train somewhere late in the afternoon, there had been a murderous brawl, and a man had been stabbed. Meredith saw nothing of the incident but heard plenty. The story moved quickly up the line as their momentum stalled. The young man stabbed had died within the hour. There was loud crying. Someone's heart was breaking.

"I thought we got rid of the troublemakers," whispered Mrs. Raymond, Meredith's neighbor on the next wagon and the woman Meredith had come to know quite well.

That night in the harsh glare of a roaring bonfire, except for a few women chosen to look after the children, all adults were forced to be in attendance for the trial of the young man. Many of the men, most in fact, did not want to serve on the jury but they had no choice Chandler told them. He conducted a quick trial, three witnesses after swearing to be truthful by placing their hands on the Bible, told what they saw. The accused had grabbed the victim and had been punched and had drawn a knife and drawn it across the victim's throat causing the poor man to bleed to death in front of his family. It was, they all agreed, murder. The young Irishman responsible for the stabbing was not much older than Meredith. His young wife was frantic, crying, lashing out at Chandler, then verbally and once, breaking away and physically attacking the white-faced jury. The two outriders physically picked her up and carried her off, so the trail could continue. After listening to the testimony, the jury found the Irishman guilty. It was martial law: wartime law. The law of the trial.

As they set about to hang the convicted man, the young wife broke away once more running into their midst, cursing and damning them all. Her intense lament rang through the woods.

"Goddamn you, goddamn you to hell."

Chandler doubled the guard.

Thankfully, Meredith didn't have to watch the execution. Women were excused. But not the men; they were made to watch as a moral lesson. Some didn't need to be commanded. They were quite eager to witness something they considered exciting. Some men brought their children to watch. A lesson they would remember of the wages of sin. Some just considered the execution a diversion from the grinding, grueling journey in a desolate, dangerous wilderness.

A pall of silence settled over the travelers. They lumbered along corduroy roads, cow pastures, footpaths, and valleys with a sense of foreboding. Twice Indians appeared on high ridges above them. *"They are Shawnee,"* Chandler declared after an examination with his spyglass. He said there was nothing to worry about. Nonetheless, flintlocks and repeating rifles were held tighter. The additional precautions kept Billy sitting up front, riding shotgun next to the potter. It gave Meredith some badly needed breathing space. She and Mrs. Raymond would walk by the hour as the train dipped and rocked along.

At every farm, at every hovel, Meredith inquired about her brother. They forded a river one afternoon and came upon a dozen people around a campfire. That is when, astoundingly, there came a blind, almost impossible stroke of luck. The two families camped around the open fire had been living in eastern Tennessee. Yes, there was a young man who came to their farm many months ago: a young man who played the flute and could draw.

"*He did cartoons of the kids,*" one of the women said proudly, and her son, while leaving most of the family possessions behind, had saved the parchment. It was Liam's. Meredith recognized it immediately. She knew his sketching. The woman said he had stayed with them three days when they still had a farm, doing work for bed and grub.

"*He left a month before we was burned out by the Yankees. Yes, I think his name was Liam; you look a bit like him, dearie.*"

Meredith was ecstatic. He was alive out there somewhere, ahead of her by many miles, but alive bound either south or west. California was a place Liam had talked about. Dear God, he was alive. "*Yes,*" said the weary woman from Tennessee, "*that is him,*" on hearing Meredith's description."

Meredith's happiness bubbled over. Regena Raymond listened intently as a joyful Meredith told her the news. "*My dear, at least you know he's alive.*"

Regena and Meredith had become close. The Raymonds had lost four children to smallpox and had left England for a new life in America. They had just built a home across the river from Washington when cannon from the Battle of Bull Run had blown the front of their new home to splinters.

"*Of course, the war wasn't a consideration when we started building our house. We had no idea there was such a simmering hatred in our new homeland. Oh, the politicians were blathering on just as they do in England, but really we were settling and building, and then came the fighting. What could we do? They were fighting on our doorstep.*"

That night wrapped in her bedroll Meredith stayed under the stars despite Billy and his grumbling that she should come under the wagon because it was going to rain. There was not a sign of rain. The sky was clear and vast, and Meredith searched the heavens for some answer as to why she was continuing the search. Liam was alive and not even bothering to change his name. Was that not enough? Could she not be released from this mission? What would Vena do if she learned her daughter had called it quits? Send someone else. It would have to be Jacob or maybe Janet, certainly not poor damaged Sarah. The twins were too young. Maybe her mother would go herself. No, she could not leave Clifton and the twins and Sarah. Liam was ahead of her, but he seemed to be taking his time, seemingly unfazed about being caught.

Meredith realized once again she had failed to ask pertinent questions. Was he still in uniform? Did he appear healthy? Had he been wounded or injured in any way? Why did she not ask? Stupid. Why would a man on the run from the Federal army of the United States dawdle across the country? A deserter in no particular hurry. A man who, if caught, could be court martialed for his crime or, at the very least, be ordered back into the army. Some deserters were shot. Meredith thought about everything she had heard. It was the flute playing that she mostly hung to. Yes, many men played the flute. But the woman from Tennessee said the young man with flaxen hair, who called himself Liam, played beautifully. Not so many did that.

Billy nodded when she told him the news. He was unhappy. Meredith could see that and tried to get him to talk. Finally, as usual, it came pouring out of him the way things always did. He didn't like McCarthy. He didn't like Mrs. Raymond, didn't like Chandler, didn't trust those crazy Irishmen, and their snotty-nosed nippers with their constant wailing. The cursing of the wife of the executed man was on his nerves too. *"She is casting a pall over all of us. Let's leave and get away from these people."* Meredith realized it had been a mistake to ask him to accompany her. She had been overcome emotionally by his hurt and heartache. But the bond between them was wearing thin. Yet, she could not even heavily chastise him because he was so kind to her in many ways.

In the evening, most people sat around the dozen fires drinking coffee and chatting among themselves. Billy sat next to Meredith sharpening his knife and glaring wickedly at McCarthy. The potter seemed not to notice or care. The next day Meredith told Billy to put his knife away and stop acting in such a threatening manner. Again, he pleaded with Meredith to leave with him.

"And go where Billy? Wander off into the woods? I will not leave, and neither will you."

Meredith realized that Billy was more damaged by the war than she had initially suspected. He was acting dangerously. In Nashville, they would have to part company. She also knew she would have to haul up in Nashville for some considerable time. It meant saying good-bye to Regena and the potter and, yes, to Billy too. She needed to correspond with her mother and explain that Liam was alive. Also, she had notes on the trial that required time to compose articles for the Clarks' and to await their replies. Her letter home would be the best news possible for her mother. That gave her some comfort. Meredith needed news too. Suppose Liam had not gone west but had returned to Nova Scotia? It was doubtful, but Liam could be highly unpredictable. She hoped and prayed that was the case and that he was home and safe. A wonderful thought, but she didn't really believe it. Meredith felt from Liam's point of view, the bond with his mother was permanently broken. Meredith knew her brother really didn't understand the horrible sadness he was putting on his family. Vena had been cruel to him. Crazy and cruel. Liam, while not cruel himself, could use a rhyme or song to tease you. Of course, that killing, which Liam had described as murder. What had that done to him?

The following day, Mr. Chandler reorganized the wagons to separate the feuding parties. Two wagons were brought up from the back of the caravan and put close to the front of the train between the potter and the Raymond's. Except at mealtimes, Meredith seldom saw the Scottish lady from the boarding house in Falmouth. The hen, as Meredith thought of her, and her husband had been at least three dozen wagons away. They had never shared the same fire for cooking and did not acknowledge each other. Now the Scottish woman was in the wagon right behind her. She briskly came up and introduced herself as Pauline McKendrick. No mention of the boarding house. They were traveling neighbors now sharing the same fire and in the same group walking.

If Billy didn't like the kind, genteel manners of soft-spoken Regena Raymond, he absolutely despised the sharp-tongued Pauline McKendrick. At their first shared cooking fire, she told Billy he was not up to much if that's all the firewood he could find. Meredith suspected Billy had never encountered anyone like this woman. She was so outspoken and direct. Giving a piece of her mind to the wagon master when she thought it was required. And she a mere paying passenger and no wagon proprietor.

Pauline had a strength to her. It was an internal force that showed no fear, and despite her initial misgivings, Meredith had to admit it was a quality to admire. Pauline was bossy but bossy to everyone, so there was a less personal sting to her comments. Besides, when Meredith walked with Pauline, Billy kept his distance. The same during the evening meal. When Pauline sat down next to Meredith, Billy stayed away and glared across the fire.

In the long hours that made up their days, Meredith became less guarded of Pauline, and the two women began to confide in each other. Slowly over the miles and evenings around the fire, they learned the depth of one another. Even better understood was their similar relationships with their mothers. What better way to understand things than to explain them to someone who asked prying questions?

"You should be a journalist," Meredith told her, and Pauline simply put back her head and roared.

"My language would be too rough. My education was interrupted."

"For what reason?" asked Meredith, never missing an opportunity for the quick verbal thrust as practiced by her new friend.

"My sponsor felt one too many derrieres." Meredith looked at her, and both women broke out laughing.

When Pauline McKendrick told Meredith she was on a fool's errand, Meredith agreed. She said the articles for the magazine and the journal she kept made the mission worthwhile. Yet, secretly, Meredith didn't really believe it. Deep within her, she sensed something else. Something she kept to herself. Something she had not revealed to Regena Raymond. She knew things other people didn't. Liam was alive: she felt it. She was confident he was moving west. As children, they talked by the hour of their dreams, the places they wanted to visit. For Liam, it was always the great cities of Europe and the coast of California. For Europe, he would need a ship, and the Atlantic coast was completely controlled by the Federal Navy. With no funds for passage and too many unionists, she believed he would strike out for California. She would check exhaustively in Nashville. But she didn't expect to find him there. Then she suspected she would keep going.

"*Do you remember the first time we met?*" Meredith asked Pauline McKendrick one day after they were very comfortable with each other.

Pauline didn't until reminded of the Falmouth boarding house.

"*Did you know you took my pork chop,*" Meredith said with a twinkle in her eye.

"*Ah, now I do. You were the girl who went without her pork chop. Yes, that was you. I remember I left you speechless.*"

"*Well, I always wondered,*" Meredith said after a pause, "*Why did you do that?*"

"*Why?*"

"*Yes, why? What was the reason for stealing my pork chop?*"

"*The oldest reason in the world, dear lassie. I was hungry.*"

Pauline was a survivor. She was frank and truthful, and Meredith grudgingly admitted she had learned a few things from her. Her interviewing skills would be improved with her ability to ask more direct pointed questions. Also, more importantly, Meredith understood she should never be so quick to pass judgment on someone, even if they do steal her pork chop.

It started to rain. The first time in weeks, and it was a downpour. Too wet to walk. The water turned the earth into a bog, and wagons wheels punctured the soft ground. The horses worked harder, the wagons pitched and swayed more, dipping left and right, their wheels making a soft sucking sound pulling out of old ruts of long passed vehicles that had left their imprint on the earth. The ride was extremely uncomfortable for everyone. Hanging on in the back, Meredith feared she would be thrown onto the soggy ground. The horses put their heads down and pulled blindly into the downfall.

The tops of the wagons beaded droplets into small waterfalls rolling off the sides of the canvas. People wrapped their blankets around their shoulders. They were moving through a gap in the mountains. Wet rocks and a rocky path. It grew colder. Meredith wrapped herself tightly in both blankets, covering her head with them. Billy was upfront with the potter. They were having trouble with the horses. Finally, they came to a steep ridge along a slope with the track hardly wider than a footpath. The outside wheels were precariously close to the edge.

Mr. Chandler was leading the way. The travel was ponderous, their pace slow. People complained that he should hold up until the rain stopped. He bellowed at them, "*You want to be stuck here, ya damn fools, asking for an attack. We would be doomed. It might rain for a month.*" He rode off then, away from his charges to miss their complaints, keeping a watchful eye on this most dangerous passage.

The outriders, Tim and Ned, came back to report it would be another couple of hours before there was a suitable clearing. They were almost through the steep grade, the end was in sight when a wagon hit a deep rut, and with a crunching, clattering sound tipped on its side spilling its contents on the ground, including screaming women, children, and a dog. Any item that could roll did so: kettles and pots were on their way down the grade, bedding and clothing sunk in the wet earth. No one was hurt, but the youngsters were mighty scared. The worst of it was they were still on the narrow path on a very steep grade. The wagons behind could not move around the spillage. There was no room to permit passage. The contents that were not already dumped were unloaded. Chairs, kitchen supplies, and food for a family of five. It all had to be removed in the driving rain.

Meredith and the potter offered to help, but Mr. Chandler ordered the wagons that could move to keep moving. There was a clearing a few miles ahead; they were to go there and set up for the night. He ordered men to keep a watchful eye on things. Tim would go with them.

As her wagon moved away, Meredith looked through the rain at the upended vehicle and the woman holding a wailing infant who refused to be pacified. The sorrowful sight of that woman and child stayed in Meredith's memory, a harbinger of things to come.

Soggy and filled with ill-tempered people, the remaining wagons reached the clearing two hours later. It had been a dreadful day. Cooking was impossible. Some people carried bundles of dry sticks tied in canvas sacks on the sides of their wagon, but even those were wet. Except for potter McCarthy's hardtack and a mouthful of dried oatmeal, Meredith went to sleep hungry. She and Billy were beneath the wagon wrapped in pieces of canvas. Potter McCarthy squeezed into Meredith's place at the back of the wagon's box. Sometime near morning, the rain stopped. Owls hooted near dawn, and wolves began hunting. The circled wagons buzzed with the sound of soft snoring. Everyone was exhausted. Meredith rose and looked about, wondering what her brother was doing at that exact moment. Sleeping, she figured, what fool wasn't?

They were soon back on another narrow path through the mountains as harrowing as the day before. At least the rain had stopped, if not the misery. Potter McCarthy held the reins tightly; it was a rocky, tipsy ride. An hour into the journey, the wagon directly behind them carrying Pauline and her husband issued a sharp crack as if a flintlock had been fired. The noise brought Meredith out of her reverie. The menfolk said it was hard to believe wet wood could make such a sharp sound. They knew what it was without looking. The back axle was broken.

Although the break had caused a sharp bump to the vehicle, Pauline and her husband were unhurt. The farm couple they had hitched a ride with were shaken up. Upon seeing her tea and flour had been upset by the jolt, the woman was frantic to save what she could. On all fours, she was scooping up the valuable assets. The woman was silently weeping.

It was another unloading. Another wagon was left behind. Every item had to be removed to make the vehicle as light as possible. A fulcrum would be needed to lift the damaged wagon off the ground to replace the axle. It was a tedious job that would take hours. A dozen men pushed the broken vehicle far enough off the path for the others to squeeze by and continue. There was no waiting for a broken wagon. Tim, the outrider, was left behind to guard, and two men experienced with such work volunteered to assist with the repairs.

Pauline came up to Meredith. *"Keep a sharp eye out,"* she said and then unexpectedly hugged her. *"Keep this for me. Just in case. I have a bad feeling."*

She thrust a small diary into Meredith's hand. *"Read it if you want to. I have no secrets I need to hold back from the likes of you."*

Walking away, Pauline said over her shoulder, *"You know I am as crazy superstitious as the damn fool Irish. Keep it just in case."*

"You can come with us," Meredith replied, without asking anybody's permission. *"We could walk a while, and you could slip into my space at the back when you're tired."*

"I've been told to stay with the wagon, and I'll do it. Imagine me, will ya, doing what I'm told. Only happens once a year. Besides, I cannot leave the old dog. He needs me."

At daybreak, Chandler sent two men on horseback to see how things were progressing and determine if the broken wagons would catch up that day. He hated stragglers. The men were gone a long time. Riding back into camp, they were as white as ghosts. There was suddenly a feeling of great alarm. The men drew close to Mr. Chandler, dismounting and whispering with exaggerated motions. Seconds later, Chandler was mounted and gone with them. Many witnessed one of the riders having a few words with his wife. She staggered, requiring him to hold her. It didn't take long for the news to spread. It was vile. The expressions and gasps said as much. A young woman with child fainted unceremoniously, dropping to the ground with a thud.

Meredith heard and grabbed the back of the wagon to steady herself. She gulped in deep breaths as the landscape whirled around her. They were dead. All of them. Pauline McKendrick, her husband, the farm couple looking for a new life, the outrider Tim, the two men helping with repairs, the little children. Massacred. Murdered. The hairless, skinless orbs where their scalps had been and the blood-soaked ground covered the horrific scene. Some said the women had been violated. Their undergarments ripped to pieces, their dresses over their heads, their legs splayed. The men who found them were not neophytes to either bloodshed or violence, but even these hard-bitten men were staggered by the sight. The scene was chaos. The wagons' contents scattered and tramped underfoot. Mr. Chandler ordered a work team to bury the bodies and then move on as quickly as possible.

Meredith was severely shaken and sick at heart. Pauline, whom she had at first detested and had come to understand and admire, was dead so quickly, so suddenly. A bitterness arose from somewhere, a silent flame that burned in Meredith, and it was directed solely at her mother. Dearest mother, sitting safely on Kirk Hill, wretched as she might be. Did she have an inkling of the dangerous, erratic, dumbfounded errand on which she had dispatched her eldest daughter? Did she even care? How long must children have such unjustifiable servitude to their parents?

The bodies were wrapped and brought to the wagons, and under the evergreens, a dozen men with rifles stood guard as a hymn was sent to God during a short funeral service. In the middle of it, the wagon that had overturned the day before and required a new wheel rolled in upon them. The family who had come upon the scene of the carnage were relieved the others were still alive. Mr. Chandler declared the scalping was not any Indian he had ever seen and could have been done by any group. He was surprised they could come upon his outrider, who was diligent and an excellent shot. Tim's rifle had not been fired.

The men doffed their hats as Chandler led a prayer for the victims. An executioner only a week before, he was now a Chaplin. From hanging an Irish lad to reading from the good book, the wagon master had many jobs. Graves were dug in the soft earth by the side of the trail. Quiet men dug with their backs bent and their mouths set in grim expressions. The bodies were gently lowered with care and reverence.

Meredith had seen death up close. She had witnessed her sister's death at a tender age. Yet never had there been such a terrible day. She was a week away from her nineteenth birthday when Pauline and her husband, the Buchanan family, the young outrider Tim and men helping them, men she didn't know, went into their Kentucky graves. It was a day she would never forget. Standing near Pauline's grave, Meredith watched as wooden crosses were pounded into the ground. Pauline, who had more life in her than anyone, had slipped so quickly in and out of Meredith's life. But she had left such an impact. Was it possible that Meredith adopted such strength herself? She grasped something else too. The advice of Lewis and Clarissa, her employers in Maine, rang anew in her ears. Her literary mission had an incredible new intensity. Finding her brother was unfinished business but writing something meaningful and long lasting about this journey was suddenly so very, very important.

It was a transitional moment for Meredith McBurnie. That human transition from girl to woman, and she felt it. The group tried to sing another hymn, Oh God, our help in ages past, but rasping voices faltered and fell silent. The wagon master said another prayer, and they moved on.

Chapter 6

After the massacre, Billy let loose. Taking Meredith aside, he went into a rant concerning their situation. *"I don't like nothin' about this. Them people was murdered now we got damn Indians peeking out of the bushes at us, as well as cutthroats and irregulars from Missouri hiding in the woods. Them half-starved free slaves is popping up everywhere. I don't like none of it. I don't like that potter either. The way he keeps trying to put himself next to you. Since the murders, when them folks had their scalps cut off, you have been riding upfront with him, asking me if I don't mind walking a bit or sittin' in the back like a woman. I walk and don't say nothin'. I utter not a word of complaint cause I know you don't like it when I complain. But damn it, I don't like him at all. The free slaves, even the women and children, are making it through the countryside, and we can too. We could branch off, go cross county on our own, but you keep telling me we have to stay with the group. Fat lot of good that did that bossy Scottish woman and those with her. Tim was there to guard them. We buried him too. Me and Nick dug his grave. Mr. Chandler said, Tim's rifle was never fired. If they could sneak up and surprise Tim, what happens to the rest of us?"*

He stopped, breathless. The complaint, or most of it, was out of him. Billy gently took Meredith's hand, *"We could make it southwest. I got a compass. We would be in Nashville before the wagons."*

"No, Billy, we cannot do that."

He shook his head most vehemently, half turning away from her, *"I hate that potter fella with his stinking barrels of clay and his goddamn glazes. I'd put a knife in him as fast as you can call me a rascal. I don't like none of it."*

Meredith wanted to slap him.

"If you did such a thing, I would never speak to you again. And Mr. Billy Hunter, do not ever speak of such a dreadful thing. Do you want to get yourself executed like that poor Irishman?"

He shook his head violently.

"We could make it to Nashville instead of being hooked up with these refugees. I know you want to stop and talk to people, but there is plenty of people in Nashville."

"It is my mission Billy. Not yours. You don't have to believe in it. You could go to Washington and get your pension. You don't need to stay here. There are people we meet on the trail all the time going in the opposite direction. Hitch a ride with them."

"I ain't leaven' you." He cried, his voice full of despair. *"Besides, I hate the Yankees almost as much as I hate the rebels. If I didn't have such a grudge against my own people, I never would have got involved in this war. If Joanna hadn't died, I would have stayed out of it. All of it. But I didn't. No sirree, I was there running like a damn fool through the streets of Fredericksburg, settin' fire to them houses, watching women screaming and kids bawling and running through the snow. Some of them was in their bare feet, crying and blubbering. There was a great hullabaloo as we torched their houses and cannonballed their buildings. Flamed up that rebel town good. I did my part. Wasn't I one of the ones climbing over bodies on Prospect Hill, wishing I was dead when my foot got shot off? Yes, us Union boys lost that fight, but it weren't my fault. I was part of Franklin's Grand Division. We fought bravely. I should get some respect. Shouldn't I?"*

Meredith let him ramble, let him relieve himself of some of the pain he was feeling.

"Lieutenant Thompson saved my life. If he hadn't put that tourniquet on my leg and twisted it real tight, I would have bled to death right there in the middle of all that bloody mess. The smoke was burning my eyes. I was out of my mind and didn't even know what was happening. It was hours later when I wished I was dead. The doctor said they could not give me laudanum cause they needed it for the seriously wounded. Seriously wounded! That's what he said. Jesus Christ, I had my goddamn foot shot off. I was surprised they didn't keep me in the army. They need everyone they can get, even boys with one foot. Maybe it's just the Confederates that do that. Some of them Confederates I seen fighting was half-dead already. And look what I had to put up with. All the time in the army, I was pestered by finger-pointers cause of my southern accent. I couldn't help the way I talk. People calling me a rebel and a spy. Men in my own platoon, men I was eating, sleeping, and fighting beside. I did my share."

He had burnt himself out. Everything was changing in Billy's life. His love had been so quiet since them massacre. She had hardly spoken a word. Even when she walked with the other women, there wasn't much talking. It was only when they come across people on the trail or pass a shanty that Meredith came to life, jumping down as she did to ask questions about her brother. When she was done with her questions, she resumed her place upfront with the potter. It made Billy's blood boil.

But Billy wasn't wrong about things. James Eugene McCarthy, the forty-one-year-old potter, was noticing Meredith more than as a casual passenger. He would steal glances as she was seated next to him, writing in her journal. He admired her delicate features, her straight back, her high riding bosom, and her hair that draped so gracefully down her back. She was a beauty alright with her high cheekbones and those cool eyes that could stare into a person. She was not a woman to tell a lie to, although he figured she told a few herself. She had a force about her, a youthful, energetic determination, and the potter admired her for that. She was educated too. Carried a book of verse and a journal that, since the murders, she had written in every day.

It was so mysterious. She was traveling with a man she had passed off as her brother. The potter saw through that ruse within a week. No brother gets the moon face like that character does. When she is walking with the other women, the so-called brother keeps jumping up to watch her as if she will evaporate like mist. Meredith said she was a farm girl. But few farm girls had her poise, refinement, and elegance. Billy had country bumpkin written all over him.

It was poetry that finally caused things to unravel. On their thirty-fifth day, they reached a wide but slow-moving river. Mr. Chandler finally relented to the demands and let people pull up to the riverbank at midday to wash themselves and their clothes and rest their bones. The horses needed the rest more than the people, and there were tufts of grass in the clearing. He organized the men into hunting parties to bring in fresh game and give the women some privacy for bathing. They had twenty more days, he figured, to cover the six-hundred-mile journey.

The woods were full of game, and all three hunting parties were successful. They roasted venison, pheasant, and trout too that the older children had caught. In the early evening, a couple of wagon drivers got out a fiddle and a squeezebox. Music rekindled a bit of spirit in the group. There was even laughter as people sat around the three big fires singing and telling tall tales that nobody believed but enjoyed anyway. It was the best day since the murders.

Meredith had been writing in her journal, her hand, and graphite gliding over the rough page with a grace that potter McCarthy so admired. When she finished and put away her journal, she took out her book of verse. She was sitting on canvas between Billy and the potter, both men as close to her as they dared to be.

"Would you do me the courtesy of reading me something?" The potter said, ignoring as he always did, the cold stare Billy was fixing on him.

She read Keats, "*Ode to a Nightingale.*"

'My heart aches, and a drowsy numbness pains,
My sense, as though of hemlock I had drunk,
Or emptied some dull opiate to the drains,
One minute past, and Lethe-wards had sunk:
'Tis not through envy of thy happy lot,
But being too happy...'

That's as far as she got. Billy could stand no more. He jumped up and, with a flash of his blade, opened the potter's forehead in a great gaping wound. Blood spilled like a mountain waterfall covering the potter's face. Billy leaned over his victim, ready for another, more deadly plunge but Meredith, still sitting, put both feet into Billy's stomach knocked him backward.

Nearby, people were already upon Billy. He slashed the air, forcing the blood to flee, his blade splattering those nearby. He whirled about those trying to contain him. His stance wide, his face covered in sweat, madness in his eyes, his knife ever moving and threatening. No man moved to disarm him.

"*Where's Chandler,*" someone cried. "*This is the wagon master's job.*"

Billy didn't wait. He latched onto Meredith's wrist and roughly yanked her to her feet. "*Come on,*" he cried and pulled her behind him.

"*Billy, no,*" she pleaded repeatedly. He was dragging her out of the wagon circle into the darkness along the river. She begged him to stop, but he would not. Stumbling, she fell. He pulled her to her feet again, and when she fell a second time, he dragged her along the ground. She had to do something. Stumbling, she felt the ground with her free hand. The riverbank was rocky, and when she got to her feet the next time, she held a rock. Regaining her footing, she struck Billy hard. It was he who stumbled, trying to drag her up the shallow bank into nearby woods. Meredith broke his grip, and she stood away from him, panting and in pain. Her knee was bleeding. She could feel warm blood trickling down her leg. It was of no concern. There was the potter's blood on her face from Billy's blade, it was of no concern. Nor was the ache in her arm or the bruise gathering substantially on her forehead.

Out of breath with the rock still in her hand, she tried to make her words soft and caring.

"Billy, what have you done? What are you doing? Why? Why? Why did you stab…"

Already she heard the clatter of horses along the riverbank. Mr. Chandler and other riders were behind them.

"I love you."

That was all Billy said before disappearing up the bank and into the bush.

"Where is he?" Chandler roughly demanded as he stopped his horse before her.

She pointed. But it was not in the direction Billy had gone. Instead, she let them believe he had moved farther along the river. They passed her, working their horses around the uprooted trees, cottonwood stumps, and boulders on the river's edge.

Shaken, unsteady on her feet, knowing that before long, Chandler would discover her deception. If they didn't find Billy tonight, he would be back in the morning with his hounds. He would find Billy's trail through the bush. He was that kind of man.

Her knee was bleeding, her arm ached from Bill pulling and then dragging her. Meredith stopped twice to catch her breath. The second time, she saw her dress was torn. She reached the wagons and collapsed into the arms of Regena Raymond.

"You poor girl. You are like my daughter. Oh dear, God in heaven, are you injured?" Regena administered to Meredith, putting salve on the deep gash below her knee. She would miss Meredith when they parted in Nashville, but Regena understood why the young woman felt she must remain there for the sake of her correspondence. She was such a bright girl, but Billy was a bad one. Regena believed that from the very first moment she laid eyes on him. She never could understand why they were traveling together. Meredith was rather refined, and he was a complete bumpkin without decent

manners. Poor lass is on a fool's mission too. She will fail, yet she is so true to her family, so determined that at every turn, she makes inquiries. People look at her in bewilderment. What kind of woman in front of perfect strangers unburdens herself and makes such outlandish inquiries? Regena saw Meredith as a diligent sister devoted to her family. Myra, her eldest daughter, would be Meredith's age had she lived. It is unfortunate Meredith is leaving. I will miss our talks together. At least she will be free of that Billy, who will be hunted down and arrested. My dearest girl, how I shall miss you and our conversations.

She was in a frenzy. Talking to herself while tending to the injured knee and putting a cold cloth on the rising bump on Meredith's forehead. Some of the women were administering to the potter with a towel on his forehead. His bleeding had mostly stopped, and he was conscious.

"Are you alright?" he asked when Meredith hobbled over to him. She suddenly felt so exhausted all she could say was,

"I'm sorry."

And she was so very sorry. Sorry for the potter and the gash across his forehead. Sorry for Billy being chased down and maybe killed in the bush. Sorry for herself. Sorry for her brother. Sorry for the war and the entire human race.

Mr. Chandler and the three riders with him came back empty-handed. He would go again at daybreak with his dogs. He took Billy's shirt for his Wolfhounds to sniff. He was indifferent to the potter or Meredith.

"I knew he was in love with you," the potter said, *"but he was not a suitable man for a woman like yourself."* Meredith gave him a cool appraisal. *"Unlike most maidens, I'm not looking for a husband. I have a mission of importance. I have a position with a magazine in Maine. I have plans that do not at this time include attachment."*

Even to her own ears, she sounded pontifical. Was that why the potter, despite his wound, was smiling at her. Was it sympathy or her comedic nature? He raised up on an elbow. *"I'm unsure I can handle the reins,"* she told him not to worry. If it was necessary, she could drive the horses. *"I was on the hay wagon since I was seven. We had a small farm. Everybody worked."*

Meredith watched Mr. Chandler and his Wolfhounds leave camp at sunrise, and a shiver ran through her. She heard him giving orders to some of the wagon drivers. He would not leave them for long. He would search for Billy for half a day, but his duty was to the wagon train.

The wagons moved out. Rifles at the ready. Six hours later, Chandler and his dogs were back. They did not have Billy. He gave Meredith a sharp eye as he passed but said nothing. How does a man with a wooden foot escape? How does such a man outrun a horse and the dogs?

Chapter 7

The wagon train was much diminished when it finally rolled into Nashville. The original fifty-six wagons now numbered forty-four. There was no fanfare to celebrate their arrival. They were, in fact, not much noticed, just another bunch of strangers going somewhere. The streets were full of livestock and horses. Flags of the United States were on many buildings: the occupation of Nashville was not to be missed. Freight wagons, military limbers, fancy gigs, four-horse rigs, and expensive landaus passed by. Men covered in sweat unloaded big-wheeled freight wagons on both sides of the street, shouldering puncheons and rolling barrels of flour and sugar as merchants stood by the door taking inventory. Drovers and cattlemen dogged along at a constant pace, their shirts carrying the dirt of the trail. Fancy-suited gentlemen ignored all such lowbrow pursuits.

Union officers were everywhere, their blue uniforms breaking up the civilian dress. There were black men smartly marching in the same uniform. Refusing to acknowledge them were southern women with dresses sweeping the ground, and shopping baskets held high in their search for butter and corn. Public ladies paraded by in silk dresses and fancy hats adorned by long feathers of white and pink. They flounced two abreast and sometimes in threes, their hat feathers bobbing above them as if a bevy of doves were about to descend.

The hustle, bustle, and clatter of commercial activity made a low rumble. Unionists and Confederate sympathizers had collected in Nashville to spy and, of course, do business because there was always business to be done. Often these occupations were conducted simultaneously. Businessmen in felt hats from the north seemed to be everywhere. They were easy to pick out, and the New Yorkers, that awful manner of speech. Meredith and the potter soon met charming carpet beggars from Connecticut and a Baltimore blockade runner who informed Meredith, confidentially, after taking her aside that the city was teeming with spies and conspirators working for themselves and one side or the other or sometimes both sides. Mostly Meredith saw one-legged veterans trying their hand at begging and men with missing arms selling apples. Nashville had been under federal occupation for two years. It was secure, the United States government owned the Tennessee River. Nashville was safe. A perfect nest for those looking for a quick dollar and for information.

Atop her perch, in the wagon, Meredith noticed how the fashionable women held their heads higher walking among the blacks. The painted women were louder and paid no attention to any of them and totally ignored the snubs tossed their way. *"Hooker's girls,"* potter McCarthy said, but Meredith would soon learn in Tennessee, they were often referred to as fallen doves. Down a side street, a platoon of black soldiers was marching. Their smart army blues looked new. A sergeant was at their side bellowing Step One-Two in quick succession. Horse soldiers followed and Indian scouts wrapped in blankets behind them. Children sat on the wooden sidewalks with little dogs. Nashville was the hub of the war, and the economic pace was accelerating.

Before the first day was over, the potter offered Meredith an opportunity, *"Stay with me until I'm better,"* he pleaded. Meredith agreed but for only a short time. She was uncertain whether he really needed her to help him and was not just playing on her sympathies or possibly for other reasons. Their first task was to find suitable arrangements. The town was full, and it took several hours to secure lodging. The wagon train was soon moving on, but Meredith was staying put, and Potter McCarthy had reached his desired destination. Where else was business as thriving as here? He was ready to set up shop and requested Meredith to escort him in his search for suitable business property.

"I require a location in the central business district where plenty of people pass by and admire my work. Can you design an advertisement for the newspapers?"

Thus began her position as the potter's assistant. She made the rounds of newspapers each week with advertisements announcing the establishment of a new pottery shop. She made the rounds of the army headquarters, too, inquiring about her brother.

The army offered little encouragement. Some of the union officers were gruff and said they had no time to waste on deserters. As far as they were concerned, all deserters should be shot. Only one ordinance corporal checked the list of prisoners. There was a Liam of the right age and, after much pleading, reluctantly he was brought before her. He was an Irish lad from Dublin who told Meredith he had come to America for a better life and had not found it. Meredith wanted to cry. She felt so sorry for the young man and asked him if she could do anything for him, but the corporal interrupted, telling her she could not console and comfort deserters. "*They need their hides whipped,*" he repeated, and the young man was roughly returned to the Provost guards.

The search with the potter taught Meredith the main streets of Nashville. The little shop they found was on Duncan Street. It had been vacated by a milliner who sought larger premises. The shop was long and narrow but contained a large window that covered most of the front. Meredith had a tiny room at the very back next to the kiln and warm enough to her liking. Potter McCarthy slept in the shop, curled up under the counter. He set to work early, and Meredith assisted him, mixing paints and glazes. When the first pieces came out of the kiln, she helped with the painting and enjoyed the work. But Liam was very much on her mind. What wonders he could do in such an occupation as painting. Within weeks the shop window was filling up with beautiful little bowls and vases. They managed to jointly work and co-habituate in such a manner for two months. Meredith spent the evenings stooped over her lantern when the shop work was done, writing in her journal and completing articles on her travels and observations. She detailed daily life on the wagon train, the challenges, the nightly fires, and food preparation. She described the battlefields and the homeless people: the bands of wandering human remnants of war. She described the villages burned, and farms deserted. The rootless free slaves. She wrote of the red Indians who refused to trust or even talk to her. She told in one dispatch of the thousands pouring into Nashville. She wrote of the transient population needing work and that Nashville offered jobs in its depots, warehouses, and wharves. In its hospitals too.

Nashville provided something else as well -- safety. Many stayed because the countryside was dangerous.

Meredith wanted to write Regena, but no one knew where in Colorado or farther west Regena and her husband would end up. They had no fixed destination in mind. They just wanted to be far away from the war. Regena did not care for the potter and warned Meredith to be very cautious around him. Meredith wondered about Billy too. If he had been shot by Mr. Chandler, would his body just be left for the animals to devour? So many things unsettled her, and one was the potter himself. Regena might have been right about him. With both Meredith's friend and Billy out of her life, McCarthy began with subtle hints. He started telling her they were a great couple and slowly started making more strident advances. Once or twice a week, he would brush up against her. Then the contact became more provocative. One night he threw caution to the wind and tried to embrace her. Meredith told him flatly to leave her be. He would do so for a while: a week or two, then, as if driven by some secret impulse, he would act less than a gentleman. She finally insulted him, told him he was too old and she was not interested, and if she wanted romance, she would seek a younger man. That stung. The evidence was in his eyes. Aside from his unwanted flirtations, when he was totally engaged in his craft, they got along well.

Outside the shop, Meredith found the pace and tempo of Nashville to her liking. She took the air at mid-mornings and in the evenings when the pulse of Nashville beat the fastest. She would walk down Second Ave to Stockyard Blvd., and sometimes she would go as far as Murfreelos Park. The rapid pace of things energized her journalistic drive. She often tried to interview people. Some co-operated, flattered to be asked questions. Others considered her bold and told her so. Some considered her a spy. One man spat at her when she told him she was from Maine. *"Yankee whore,"* He uttered.

"I am no such thing." She withdrew to the shop and stayed there the remainder of the day, condemning herself with mutterings about her cowardice. She wanted to be taken seriously. To report more deeply, make her articles insightful and authentic about the war, the south, and confederate cities under federal control. She needed to talk to people from different walks of life. Meredith wanted to know and see it all. She

wanted to write about daily life in the Confederacy, the black regiments in the Union Army, and how public women had lost their moral compass.

There was the danger, people would consider such writing improper, yet she was fascinated with the loose morals suddenly surrounding her. The flourishing red-light district was something she had never dreamed of. Was it the war? It was so different from strait-laced Nova Scotia or prim Portland. There was nothing that compared to what she witnessed every day. Would her employers publish such stories? Richard would not, but Clarissa might if she saw the point of it. She was braver than her husband, and Meredith wanted to dig beneath the surface to discover the societal changes brought about by this great conflict. The poverty, the desperation that changed people. She firmly believed there were solid identifiable reasons people gave themselves over to the devil. Were they downtrodden in spirit, or was it just the greed of easy money? If she could write about such people, raise them up, make them human, it might touch readers. People were so ready to condemn those they did not understand. Preachers shouted about sin every Sunday. Condemnation was easy from the pulpit, but what caused evil. Also, there was what she saw as the great dichotomy. Public women on the streets of Nashville did not look downtrodden. They were merry and young and seemed not in the least bothered by moral decay. But Meredith noticed on very close inspection in those women a bit older, there was less laughter as the hard-edged lines of life began to settle on their faces.

Potter McCarthy opened for business at eight in the morning and remained open until nine at night. Meredith gave some excuse to steal away for a few minutes to walk the main streets to observe the life of the city. She began to doubt herself. There was so much to learn; how could she cut through the fabric of this place to see the other side of things? She waited for her chance, and it came on a bright sunny morning when a federal officer and his wife came into the shop. He was a tall man with a pretty wife half his size. Meredith had seen few men wearing a monocle, but here was one, a European with a distinctive accent to match his eyepiece. His uniform bore the markings of a military doctor. While his wife declined assistance and just wanted to busy herself examining the potter's fine work, her husband stood stiffly at the window watching the busy street. Meredith saw it as her chance, and she took it.

75

Meredith hated lying and would feel guilty about it later. She knew she was being dishonest in fluffing up her story a bit, claiming coolly to be a writer commissioned to do a series of articles on the war and life in the south. He seemed to bristle at her initial approach, straightening up, becoming taller, and giving her a stern gaze. Meredith kept pressing. Would it be possible, she wondered, for her to interview him and maybe accompany him on his rounds so her readers could learn of the important work doctors were doing here? Union doctors, of course. The question was never answered. Potter McCarthy, interrupted, practically shooing Meredith away.

"What are you doing?" He asked her when the shop was empty. His tone was one she did not care for.

"I'm trying to find a story. I've already written about the quick life of Nashville. I need to delve into these people. The doctor, if he would help me, could be of great assistance."

"Do you think I want you to be around disease and pestilence and then come into my shop and wait on customers?" His rebuke made her laugh out loud. The entire city was full of disease and pestilence. Painted ladies were in the shop the moment the doors opened. They didn't buy; they just gleefully looked and left, always in twos or threes. But the doctor was standing alone. Why shouldn't she approach him? The potters' criticism was a ruse to control her, and she knew it. *"Mr. McCarthy, I am neither your child nor your responsibility. I would ask you not to interfere with my journalistic intentions."*

"That customer, that doctor, he was uncomfortable by your advances."

"They were professional advances, I assure you."

"I don't want you harassing the customers."

"Then I shall leave and find lodging and employment elsewhere."

"Please don't talk like that. I need you here with me. I am still unwell," he said, touching the healing wound on his forehead. *"I have headaches from the knife wound your beau gave me."* He softened his tone. *"You are a tremendous assistance."*

"He was not my beau, as you very well know."

Meredith thought for a moment. *"Let us make a compromise. I will open the shop and work till mid-afternoon. The rest of the day, I pursue my own writing."*

He didn't like it one bit. But, after a blustering tirade and repeated arguments that went on the next hour, he finally relented. But there was a penalty to pay; Meredith's wages were reduced from seventy-five to sixty cents a day.

An hour later, he apologized for his abruptness and manners and took her to dinner that night to seal their new bargain. She feared he might use the occasion to propose marriage but, much to her relief, he did not.

Over the next several days, she kept an eye out for the doctor with the heavy accent, but it was he who found her. Returning from an errand one morning, he was waiting in the pottery shop.

"Are you a scribbler, or are you a shop-girl?" He demanded without introduction.

"I'm a writer, traveling by wagon train, working in shops, riding the rails and footpaths of this country to report on the stories of the war and its people."

She got it out all in one sentence and felt it was a good response, at least until she saw the disapproving face of potter McCarthy, scurrying around watching them as a chicken hawk watches potential prey.

"May we walk a spell," she inquired, and the doctor gave a curt nod indicating consent.

He took her to a tea house where he informed her she was too young to be a scribbler of any importance. Then he launched into a dissertation of his vital work and inquired briskly why she wasn't writing down his comments.

"I'd like to just talk at first, then I'll do a proper interview with you if you are agreeable." He was more than agreeable. It didn't take Meredith long to understand the doctor had his own agenda. What he sought was personal fame and saw Meredith as an opportunity to further his ambitions. He did all the talking and at one point brought up the subject of the city's prostitutes who interfere with his more important work by taking up too much of his time.

"The whores are a real bother. Union wartime regulations force them on me. They must be inspected and purchase a license, something they are not too happy about, and neither am I. General Rosecrans made the ruling to protect soldiers from venereal disease."

She was certain he would let her write all she wanted about him, and she was right.

"I save lives. The generals lose lives. So, I ask you who is of better service to humanity? Don't write that, not about the general, just write I save hundreds no, no, thousands of lives at great personal risk to myself."

"I not only want to write it, but I also want to see you at work."

77

"But of course, tomorrow we will go to the hospital. You shall see it all, but write it down scribbler, there is too much for your memory."

He was Hungarian. She had no experience with Europeans except for a few Dutch families in the wagon train. She wondered if all Hungarians were as egotistical as this man with his abrupt manner and his monocle. They agreed to meet the following morning at nine. He told her not to forget her graphite and writing journal.

"You will see much."

His name was Von Hicklestien. German first, then Hungarian, now American. *"I have had a most interesting life, as you shall see,"* he informed her on their parting.

She thought him a buffoon, yet he opened a door for her, a new avenue for her writing. This was what she had been looking for.

Potter McCarthy was furious. She was hired to tend shop not to go running off the first chance she got. Meredith seemed to be reliving her recent past. The potter was replacing Billy. Trying to contain her. At first, Meredith tried to placate him, she would make up the hours. *"No,"* he said that was not good enough. They argued, and she would not give in to his wishes. When nothing else worked, he tried to scare her.

"I have been talking to some of the other merchants. This is not as safe a city as you believe it to be. A secret Confederate underground is operating; they are smuggling arms, medicines, and spying for the Confederacy. These are dangerous men, yet you go traipsing around by yourself, free as a bird."

She would not be deterred, and it evolved into a bitter exchange of words, resulting in Meredith retiring to her room and the potter refusing to leave her alone, alternating between bullying and beseeching.

"You are young and foolish. Totally foolish. Listen to me. I know what I'm talking about. You're asking for trouble going off with strangers. I want you here."

When bulling didn't work, he tried pleading.

"Why will you not allow me to protect you? I am willing to give you everything. I would lay down my life for you. I could not work today when you went off with that officer, I ruined two pieces in a row."

"I am not in need of protection, nor do I desire your possessions."

"Why can't you be gracious instead of throwing my offer back in my face. You are most heartless, more like a witch than a pretty young woman."

He became enraged and shook his fist at her and kicked the wall in frustration. The gash from Billy's knife now flushed purple. When he grabbed her, she pushed him away. He raised his fist in a threatening manner as if to strike her. There was real anger in his eyes. Meredith glared back at him, and he backed down and continually apologized. Meredith grabbed her possessions, and when the potter saw what she was doing, he berated her again until hurriedly, she fled into the dark and dangerous Nashville night. When he violently slammed the door behind her, it resembled the sharp crack of a rifle. For Meredith, it was potter McCarthy's last act of aggression.

Chapter 8

The decrepit hotel was next to a saloon called Rosie's. Walking by the doors, a passerby could see the garish paintings on the walls. Large paintings of horses and half-dressed women. But the hotel had the cheapest rooms. The proprietor could afford to offer such a bargain as many rooms were used for an hour or less. Meredith put the pillow over her head to block out the disturbance coming through the walls. Down the hall, two men and a woman were engaged in a boisterous argument. On the other side, a woman was squealing in intimate delight. With the pillow held tightly to her ears, Meredith's mind was churning from the potter's anger, the doctor's bluster, the fruitless search for Liam, and the three articles she had sent to the Clarks, and two more she had not yet completed. Her life was suddenly terribly exhausting. But surprisingly, considering the state of her agitation, she eventually fell into a deep sleep.

She awoke with a start, already late for their meeting. The doctor was still standing at the corner of the street where they agreed to meet at nine sharp, not ten after. Giving her a critical look, he said nothing but, *"Good Morning,"* and waved away her excuses for tardiness. They walked briskly past dry goods stores, a chandler, a harness maker, and a small booth with a sign that indicated your fortune could be told for two bits. Soon they arrived at his hospital. Before the war, the building had been a warehouse, its timbers untouched by past hostilities.

In stepping through the front doors, Meredith was surprised at the cleanliness. Compared to the dusty streets and tattered appearance of a quickly swelling city, the hospital's interior had a gleaming purity about it. The air was heavy with soapy acid smells. There was a good deal of silent hurrying and scurrying, up and down rows of beds containing bandaged men. The army nurses and volunteers moved with quiet efficiency. When Meredith remarked on the cleanliness, including the white bed sheets, the doctor raised his hand to stop her. *"We have learned in recent years that sanitary conditions prevent the spread of disease. It is as much infection as bullets that kills. I myself have educated others in my profession on this correct course. Are you taking this down?"*

They walked by different wards separated by bed sheets. Grim-faced men looked back at them, but most were asleep or unconscious. *"We separate now, all those needing leg amputations in one area, those suffering from gut wounds in another area. These men suffer from typhus. Similar afflictions are kept together. Treatment is easier that way. There is less confusion. Come to our operating theater."*

The theater had been a shipping office. A half dozen men were observing a young doctor.

"Ah, good morning Doctor Sanford. What are we doing today?"

"Removing a bullet from the chest cavity," Dr. Sanford replied without looking up.

Spellbound, Meredith watched the procedure, but the constant probing and the blood finally made her queasy. She had overslept and had not eaten breakfast. Come to think of it, she had missed supper too. Meredith stiffened herself and closed her eyes until Dr. Von Hicklestien simply said, *"Come,"* and they walked off.

"You are unwell, Miss Scribbler?"

"I'm fine, just dizzy. I haven't eaten since yesterday."

A chow tent was behind the hospital. The fresh air felt good on her face, but as they walked to the back of the long building, they passed an unusual pile of what appeared to be cordwood. For some strange reason, it was covered in blood. To Meredith's abject horror, upon closer inspection, it was a stack of amputated limbs. She considered taking hold of the doctor to steady herself but didn't. *"Yes,"* he said, *"there are many amputations."*

Over barley soup and a plate of beans, he described in lurid detail how he had revolutionized the treatment of men in wartime conditions. *"My procedures will outlast the war. Believe me when I tell it. That man having the bullet removed from his chest was unconscious due to our use of ether. Ether, that wasn't available in the Mexican war. No, not at all. Back then, they put a piece of rawhide in the patient's mouth and sawed away until the patient fainted from the pain. Ether has been a great improvement, and I am responsible for bringing it into modern medicine. Why aren't you taking notes, Miss Scribbler?"*

She made notes. Plenty of notes, despite his constant inquiries, if she was writing everything down as if, she thought to herself, one of his pearls might escape her attention. When they returned to the hospital, the pile of amputated limbs was gone. At least she thought they were gone, but in truth, she didn't look. There was a story here; certainly, she just had to steel herself to stand the gore of it and the stamina to tolerate the good doctor. She watched him go about his rounds in the next few hours and learned a few things he didn't reveal. She discovered that no one at the hospital really cared for Dr. Von Hicklestien. Behind his back, they called him Doctor Carl or, more caustically, Dr. Yap-yap. Not even "Dr. Carl" was permitted in his presence. He resented personal familiarity. Meredith could see how his brisk Germanic manner, the accented speech of the European upper class grated on nerves among those toiling in the atmosphere of illness, death, and dying. He never left her alone for more than a few minutes. Once, he found her talking to a young New Yorker wrapped in head bandages and asking for water. He was proud to serve, he told her. The doctor broke up the conversation.

"It is unwise to grow attached to a patient. We have seen what happens to women, how emotionally draining it is to do that."

"I was getting him some water; I think I can do that without becoming emotionally drained."

He gave her a sharp look but said nothing. Meredith told him she wanted to talk to some of the women volunteers, but he ignored her request. *"They will know nothing."*

The wounded were arriving from some battle many miles away. Brought by train, carried to the hospital by horse and wagon. A young boy with yellow hair was dead on arrival. Some cried in anguish, wishing they were dead. Some, living their last hours, spent their time in prayer or dictating final letters of good-bye to their parents or wives and children. Meredith wrote about how people spent their final hours, about the ether and the operations, several going on at once. The sawing through bone jarred her nerves. She did not like the sucking noise of a surgeon's finger coming out of a puncture wound.

Nonetheless, the medical procedures were fascinating to observe. She faltered occasionally and ran from the scene when an eyeball was plucked from a man's head and plopped on a tin plate. The eye was staring up at her when she fled. She wrote and re-wrote an article on the hospital and another article on the operations themselves. She could take the amputations of an arm or a leg. She simply refused to observe. What was incredible and what she would write about was the magic of ether. A few drops put a man to sleep, and he would sleep through having his arm sawed off.

She tried to make conversation with the nurses and volunteers in the fleeting minutes when she was out of earshot of Dr. Von Hicklestien. There were scoffs when she mentioned the miracle he had introduced. *"Is that what he told you?"* A male army nurse asked.

By late afternoon, she felt the need to get away from the heavy atmosphere and the doctor's constant self-aggrandizing. She told him she had enough notes for one day, but he was not finished with her. They went to his workroom, which had been the office of the warehouse superintendent. There was something he wanted to demonstrate to her, something he was extremely proud of. There on the bench was the latest marvel of modern medicine. It appeared at first glance to be an amputated arm wrapped in leather. It was, he informed her, an artificial arm: another of his wondrous things. This true sign of advancement would soon go on an officer who had lost his limb at Shiloh.

"You see, Miss Scribbler; we have many marvelous advances."

"It's Meredith or Miss McBurnie, please."

"Ah, yes, yes. The Union Army of the United States introduces the newest in medicines. Those Confederates are of a lower class. You may know what I mean by saying that they use cucumbers for burns and persimmon for bowls. They are not advanced."

For some reason, she could not identify; that comment made her angry. She didn't know what made her flare up like a starving flame suddenly receiving oxygen. *"Yes, I witnessed some of the Union Army's advancement as I traveled through Fredericksburg."*

Her comment made absolutely no impact on him. In fact, he paid little attention to her questions and comments. He did the talking, and she wrote down his words. At the end of the day, he walked her back to the business district. Meredith dreaded spending another night at the hotel. She was also worried about money and decided to broach the subject with the doctor.

"Doctor Von Hicklestien, it is my intention while doing these articles on the war and the state of the union and, of course, the great advances men like yourself are making. I pledged to myself to supplement my income as I go."

He halted, bringing his foot down as if marching on a parade square. It was the first time she witnessed his total military bearing.

"Do not your employers pay you enough? You must write. I alone have much more to tell you."

To her surprise, it was the doctor who solved her problem by making his own proposal. It was not exactly what she wanted but close enough. She would work for him: not for the army or the hospital but as his personal assistant. Meredith's job was to record all his achievements, file them in an orderly fashion and turn them into a book. A book about him. He offered her two dollars a week plus room and board. She might never finish such an assignment, but it would keep her in Nashville. It would give her a base to communicate with her family and keep poking around the army looking for Liam. She would have been delighted to know that money was already on its way to her from the Clark's in Portland and her mother in Nova Scotia.

So as the months rolled by and summer turned to autumn, and a new nip in the air ushered in 1865, Meredith was the doctor's lap dog. Following her master hour after numbing hour, through antiseptic wards, never failing to scribble his various accomplishments. The staff watched her skeptically, and when the doctor disappeared for a minute or two, and it was safe, they approached her with questions.

"What are you writing?" It gave her the very brief opportunity to talk to them, although such opportunities were always cut short as the doctor wanted his new scribbling servant constantly by his side. She slept in his office on an army cot at night and took her meals in the mess tent. It was all-in-all an uncomfortable experience with some highly fascinating moments. To Meredith's dismay, she learned that her initial judgment of Dr. Von Hicklestien was accurate.

"He's a fraud," one of the army nurses told her. *"He takes credit he doesn't deserve. It was Dr. Letterman who brought in many of these changes, not Dr. Thumping Chest."*

Meredith smirked but said nothing. She never knew how near the doctor was and whether he was listening. He could disappear and re-appear within a minute and wiggle his finger at her to follow him. It was humiliating, but he helped her too. The doctor went to the general and asked for a complete list of all records pertaining to Union army deserters captured in Tennessee and Virginia. No prisoner by the name of Liam McBurnie had been captured or executed or mustered back into the service.

In the following weeks, Meredith received two important messages. One included a banknote for the unheard-of sum of seven dollars. The Clark's had published her story of the wagon train.

"Which we did with relish," Clarissa wrote. The other letter, she knew by its bulk, was from her mother. The envelope was thickly packed with pages. The news from home was worse. Meredith's younger brother Jacob had run off with a girl from town. Her mother had something more to be frantic about. *"What have I done to make my children hate me?"* Clifton had given up the cobbler shop. His back was a constant source of pain from too many years of bending over his workbench. There was, of course, more political nonsense at home.

"Doctor Tupper wants all schools to be publicly financed. Can you imagine? Now we have to pay for other people's children to learn their three "R's. There was still much wrangling on the move to unite all of Lower and Upper Canada, and that MacDonald fellow wants Nova Scotia to join them. Can you imagine? Nova Scotia, Upper and Lower Canada, New Brunswick, and PEI too. How silly: of course, Nova Scotia would lose the most in such a scheme. It will be the end of us. Of course, as a sop, they will no doubt name Halifax the capital of this nonsense since we have the most to lose, considering our economic superiority but really. MacDonald and Dr. Tupper run around quite willing to let the British sail off and leave us to our own defenses. I pray they will fail. We are solidly behind Mr. Howe. There is much bickering here over things and worry too. Many stories go the rounds; we even hear them here in the backwoods. People fear once the Americans stop fighting each other, they will turn on us. Dr. Tupper says we need to unite into one country, and Mr. Howe says we have the best fighting force already in Mother England."

Meredith wrote her mother immediately. She reinforced her belief that Liam was alive. Again, she volunteered to come home to help the family. Her hand trembled as she wrote those words. She did not want to return to Nova Scotia, fearing, as Liam had, that once she returned, she would never get away again. The Clarks were publishing her stories. She had a great craving to write. Even to stay on this crazy journey and write about what she saw: Nashville, the hospital, the public ladies. So many people and stories. But if it must all be put aside, well, so be it. She would wait for word, and if the message was, come home, she would do it. *"I will wait for your reply, but if you say come home, I will do so willingly."*

Regardless of her mother's reply, she would one day write a book. Not about the doctor and his marvelous achievements but about Liam and her search for him. Meredith McBurnie was nineteen years and already knew what a good, solid story was. She also knew she was living such a story.

Thinking she might soon have to abandon her mission gave her more patience with the doctor. The most arduous part of her day was after supper when they would go to his office, and he would dictate long passages about his young life in Hungary to his glorious triumphs in the Mexican Wars. It was draining. She scribbled like a madwoman. One night, tired and extremely frustrated, she could take him no longer. "How does Doctor Letterman fit into this picture? Does he not have some credit?" The monocle dropped to his chest. Meredith knew the warning by his raised eyebrows.

"He has done much. But your story is not about him. It is about me. This is my story, and I am paying you to write it."

But how could she write it when everyone at the hospital said it was a sham? A lie.

Then one evening, everything changed. The doctor began running his hand up and down her spine, she objected. He was taken aback by her rejection.

"You are forgetting, doctor, that you are a married man. Your wife accompanied you to the pottery shop the first day I saw you. Your wife would not appreciate your behavior. Does she even know you are employing me?"

"It is not her business or interest whom I employ. Do not speak of her again."

"Sir, I would appreciate you keeping your hands to yourself."

He glared, grabbed his coat, and left, slamming the door, much as the potter had slammed the door a few months earlier. Meredith was dismayed. What was she doing that prompted such behavior? Why did she bring out the worst in men?

The doctor dismissed the incident. The story of his life was too important to allow a mere woman to get in the way. Again, she was his puppy dog: obediently following him through his day, note pad and graphite at hand. But the rift between them intensified when he demanded to review her notes: demanding to see everything she was writing. His temper rose when she refused. That night in his office, he pushed her against the wall with his eyes full of flint. But she would not give in. The notes were hers. As he berated her, she sank down on her cot, knowing she should, as a matter of strength, remain standing to face this man unaccustomed to having his wishes rejected. Meredith was no longer listening. The gold braids and brass buttons of his uniform were dancing before her eyes. Sputtering and glaring. It was his story; he had the right to see it. She was not scared of him, not in the least. Damn him. She was wretched not because of him or anything to do with him, as pompous and ungentlemanly as he was.

"I should never have left Maine," she said aloud, and the doctor stopped his tirade and glared more intensely. Meredith rose to her feet unsteadily. She had been in bad places before. She had seen plenty of tirades. She thought of that awful day of the lightning when her sister died. Vena McBurnie was the master of the tirade, and Meredith wondered at that moment how her soft-spoken father was handling things at home. She opened her bag and put away her notepad and graphite and left his office. She would not return, once again losing her sleeping quarters. Into the night, she walked without any direction in mind. She stood outside a saloon and removed every note she had written that day on the good doctor's young life in Hungary and his glorious triumphs in the Mexican Wars. She threw the notes into a patch of steaming horseshit. She had written all she was ever going to write about that marvelous man.

It started to rain. She leaned against a wall and fell asleep standing upright. Waking a minute later with a jolt, she returned to the hospital and the doctor's office. He had locked the door. Revenge.

Tired as she was, Meredith was not without her wits. She found the hospital's duty sergeant and informed him she was locked out of her sleeping quarters. She was in, had her clothes packed in her portmanteau, and fully dressed, fell asleep on the bed. Just after sunrise, she left the building for the last time.

The city was already beginning to wake. Some merchants were sweeping the wooden sidewalks in front of their establishments. A half dozen horsemen rode by. A few ladies of the night staggered past, stinking of cheap liquor. Then in the early morning light, Meredith saw someone she recognized.

Chapter 9

The woman was one of the whores the doctor had examined a week earlier. Meredith had witnessed the examination. The indignity of it. The women spread eagle on a table, about as demeaning as anything Meredith had ever seen. Syphilis was rampant in the army, and in the early morning light, the woman appeared even more dissipated than she had been a week ago. She was washed out, her skin splotchy. The rims around her eyes were darker. The blond hair turned to musky, tarnished brass.

Her name was Martha, which Meredith remembered because she had rebelled when she saw Meredith in the examination room. She threw a temper tantrum until the doctor's bellowing overpowered her. His explanation was Meredith was his assistant. Believing the doctor meant medical assistant Martha was somewhat mollified. She dutifully lay on the table and let him poke and even smell her. Despite the bad diagnosis, Martha took it in stride. When the examination was finished, she apologized to Meredith, and Meredith in turn squeezed Martha's hand, telling her it was alright. At the time, she wanted to engage this woman in conversation, but Von Hicklestien had been there, listening to their every word.

"We met in the doctor's office last week," Meredith said by way of introduction. Martha simply looked at her and nodded. Her eyes trying to focus. *"My cunny is still infected. They won't let me do nothing, not even the Frenchie stuff. I can't make a dollar. Could you lend me ten cents?"* Meredith bought her breakfast outside a drummer's tent. Patiently, Meredith waited. She felt certain this woman wanted to unburden herself. She appeared both ill and bursting at the seams with complaints on the insults heaped upon her. Sure enough, it wasn't long until Martha began to talk.

"These men, ya know," she shook her head. A dribble of egg yolk was on her chin, and Meredith gently wiped it away. *"Sometime they go off, ya know, too fast and they lose their hardness, and they blame me as if it's my fault they can't control themselves. They refuse to pay cause they didn't get their money's worth, or they punch me. I've been punched, kicked, thrown down a flight of stairs. Some men want to corn hole me, but I won't let them cause it hurts like hell, and they punch me cause I refuse. If I don't get paid, I got to make it up myself, and even when I do get paid, I only get to keep half the dollar I charge."*

She came from Crossbones, outside Atlanta. The daughter of a whore. Mostly raised in a brothel until the churchmen took her away at the age of nine. She had no schooling. Never knew her father but had a lot of sugar daddies along the way. Meredith found a new challenge in Martha. The interview, because that's what it was, whether Martha realized it or not, was difficult because Meredith didn't understand all she was being told. More naive than she knew or cared to admit, Meredith's questions were cumbersome, some blatantly stupid. Martha became extremely irritated when asked why she had chosen such a life.

"Chosen," the whore hissed loud enough for those around them to hear. Whore talk was common on the streets of Nashville. *"I hate this goddamned life. There was no choosing, never been any choosing, I was damned the minute I was born."*

Meredith thought Martha might leave the table in a huff, but her ravenous appetite kept her in her seat. She wasn't leaving until the cornbread was gone. It was unbelievable such a sick, pasty woman could eat so much. Martha had come to Nashville in 1862, arriving almost simultaneously with the Union Army's cannonballs.

"They were blowing things up left and right. First day I was here, the roof of the building I was walking by got blown to hell. Damn Yankees, now they control the town and most of the countryside. Knocking on old Jeff Davies door pretty soon."

After breakfast, Meredith and Martha walked to a building called the whores hospital, where Martha was supposed to be a patient.

"How do you leave; do you need a pass or something?" Martha laughed.

"We can leave if we want, but the beds are better here than sleeping outside where you can get carried into the alley by a bunch of union boys, those gallant men in blue, and you not get nothing for it. They take but don't pay. I was drinking last night and slept in a pile of hay, but I don't recommend it in this town. If I get caught working, I get a month in jail. That jail is a stink hole,

and the grub is wormy. The Yankees got more ways of sucking money out of a person. Ya know they make us buy a permit to work, and once a month we got to get inspected by that boss of yours. Five dollars for the permit to work, fifty cents for your sawbones to ram his fingers up your fair maiden. Damn Yankees. But I suppose it is better than before when they tried to get rid of us."

"How did they do that?" Meredith asked.

Martha let out a long sigh and then a yawn, and Meredith noticed half her teeth were missing. *"I will tell ya someday deary, but I got to gets some sleep. I am dog tired."*

"How about I buy you breakfast tomorrow at the same place?"

Martha gave Meredith a cold stare. *"Why you want to be seen with the likes of me. You look well enough off."* Then she moved a step closer to Meredith, *"You ain't planning for a life in this business, are you? We got enough competition already."*

Meredith stepped back, stunned by such a monstrous question but not wanting to insult the insulter.

"I am a journalist working my way across America writing about the war, the people, the suffering...."

"You cannot put suffering on a piece of paper," Martha replied, regaining her composure and standing more upright. Then she took a step back and smiled: it was the saddest smile Meredith McBurnie had ever witnessed, *"You can buy me breakfast tomorrow morning if you are not worried about your reputation, honey. I'll see you at seven."*

In the morning, Martha steered them to another hash house where she said they had good grits but later confessed her type were not permitted to hang out in one place. *"They want us moving around. Ya' know places just like people can get a name."*

"Martha, I'll be moving on soon. I am not a permanent resident of Nashville, and I am not the least bit concerned about my reputation. I have a job to accomplish, and that is what I am doing."

Without looking up from her grits and beans, Martha replied, *"Well, if you are so smart, how come you did not know about our great expedition down the Cumberland River?"*

"I haven't been in Nashville very long. Just a few months," Meredith replied. Martha didn't hear her. She had already begun her story. *"Old General Rosecrans was pulling his hair out; beside himself he was, cause nobody wanted to take us. There were too many of us public ladies, as they calls us."* She flicked her wrists as if to say la-Dee-DA. *"The union boys like us too much. The general come up with a plan to get rid of us. Get us out of Nashville ha-ha, biggest*

joke in the federal army. How was the north going to win when they can't even get rid of a bunch of whores?"

And for the first time, a tiny laugh, more mocking than funny, came out of Martha's throat. Meredith scribbled as Martha talked. People around them noticed but didn't care. In fact, those that noticed it at all considered Meredith just another one of the do-gooders and kept out of her way before she asked for a donation to her highly worthy cause. The city was full of those with worthy causes, eastern charities, abolitionists, the temperance league, the sanitation commission, etc. etc. And of course, the women who followed the army sometimes out of love and other times out of greed or more likely just mere need.

Meredith broke her graphite and grabbed her satchel for another while Martha soldiered on. *"There was too many public women in Nashville, too many soldiers getting the clap. So, the big, smart, general comes up with a plan to get rid of a load of us. We gets rounded up, them soldiers know where to find us, of course. Some they took us right off the street and emptied my house of sixteen and got forty at the house next door. He put a hundred and eleven of us on a riverboat. That boat's name was the Idaho. The boat's captain didn't want nothin' to do with us and told the general so, he would not take us up the Cumberland River to Louisville. Well the general ordered him under, ya know what they calls it."*

"Martial Law," Meredith replied.

"Ya, that's it. So the captain had no choice, and neither did we. We had no choice, they marched us on that damn boat as if we was prisoners. In fact, we were prisoners. You got on or got a baronet in the ass. It wasn't that we wanted to go or nothin' like that. Some of the girls, me included, we sneaked liquor aboard although we wasn't suppose to. The first night we was drunk as hell, the girls yelling to strangers on the riverbank, even showing off their wares. Them waving back, farm guys taking off his hat and waving it in the air. We came to a bend in the river, and two of the girls jumped overboard and swam to shore. Most of us couldn't swim, and we just hollered encouragement. The soldiers knew they lost a couple, but they didn't care. We ain't gettin' paid to go chasing no whores through the wilderness, one of them said."

Martha stopped, watching Meredith intently writing away. *"Well, when we got to Louisville, two more of the girls escaped with the help of some local boys looking for adventure. After that, somebody suddenly cared. The captain posted armed guards on deck and threatened to shoot any of us trying to get away. And here's the big joke of it, when we pulled into Louisville, the city fathers did not want us soiling their pure Lily-white citizens, although from what the girls say, they had already been soiled and soiled good. Anyway, they refused to let us off the Idaho, and them local boys that tried to take us off were threatened with arrest. By this time, the captain was fit to be tied. He never wanted to take us anyway, and he only did it cause he was ordered by General Rosecrans. Well, what could he do but move farther up river to Cincinnati. We was out of liquor by that time and feeling rotten."* She shook her head, and Meredith stopped writing and took a good look at her. Martha had a wistful look in her eyes, considering the bare existence of her life of never being wanted anywhere.

"If Louisville was bad, Cincinnati was worse. They rowed out to meet us and would not, for the love of god, even let the Idaho tie up at their precious wharf. We had to dock across the river, and no, we wasn't gettin' off there either, although Lucy and Mary sneaked away with a little help of the local boys. Them young fellas were standing on the riverbank jumpin' up and down with excitement at the offers the girls were making for a little bit of their help. What you might call a big reward. I wonder whatever happened to those girls. I never seen any of them that jumped ship."

She sighed and began again as if wanting to end the story. The pain was back in her voice.

"Whop-ti-do. Guess what? The captain brought us back here to Nashville where we started. We all about died of hunger, and we had made no money cause the crew wouldn't pay us for their pleasure."

From her hospital experience, Meredith knew that soldiers with venereal disease got treatment, mostly by silver mercury. She asked Martha if the women got the same treatment.

"I take the treatments, don't know why. I ain't gettin' better. Most of the girls just get over it, but some don't. If you got it bad, they won't even let you out of the hospital. What the hell do I care if I live or die? Does it make a difference? It don't, plain and simple. Ain't nobody to mourn."

"If I bought you breakfast every morning, would you let me talk to you, or would that be too painful for you. To talk about your life?"

Martha warned Meredith to stay away from the brothel. *"The people who run the brothel are not good. They carry knives and sometimes use them. The real owners are respectable citizens of Nashville, old southern families who hadn't been driven out by the union army. Probably because they co-operated with the occupiers."*

"Can you tell me their names?" Meredith asked.

"I don't know their names, never seen them, but I know they don't like us talking about what happens in there. Cause the people they hire, two brothers, they are rough, some bad things happen there. Girls do get murdered, and nobody ever done nothing about it. It ain't right."

Meredith was not naive enough to think she could ever sell such a story as Martha's, except maybe to a low-brow publication like the Police Gazette. Even Clarissa Clark, as liberal-minded and progressive as she was, would probably reject a story of a public woman. But it could be part of a book. Maybe. Or maybe Meredith was just reaching beyond herself. Maybe it was another pipe dream. She would write Martha's story and see where the experience took her.

That week Meredith was fortunate. She finally found a boarding house by reading the newspaper every morning. She could say good-bye to the third floor of that seedy hotel, where a few nights earlier, a woman had been stabbed to death. The same week the hospital released Martha too, but she could not work, so she was back on the street. If she could not work, she could not stay in the brothel, which was her home. Business was business. The best she could do was an empty stall at a stable. Martha said it would do, and she had slept in worse places. Meredith wished she could bring Martha to her newly acquired boarding house, which was in the heart of the city, but that was impossible. The military family living there would never permit it. From the window of her new bedroom, Meredith could see some of the buildings damaged by the fighting when federal troops captured Nashville. Her new home had large verandas and Gothic ceilings. It was occupied by Major Anthony Lovett and his wife Ester. The house had been left vacant after the owners fled when the first union cannonballs fell. More fortunate, the Lovetts had two small children, and Meredith could reduce her board by looking after the children in the afternoons, so the major's wife could rest or take tea with other military wives.

"We stick together as we are totally shunned by the southerners, not that I would want to associate with them," she sniffed.

"You must find the atmosphere rather confining?" Meredith said, and Mrs. Lovett told her exactly how awful some southerners were. *"Some of them, of course, are splendid, gentleman to the core."* Ester Lovett strolled around the room as she spoke studying Meredith from different angles. She was a tall woman with an attractive face. Her dark auburn hair was set high on her head and tied in the back. She longed for company,

she said and hoped they would become the best of friends. She had never met a writer before.

"So, Miss McBurnie, you were a teacher and gave up that calling to be a journalist? Really. That sounds like a step backward, but I suppose as a journalist, you are accustomed to frank inquiries and intelligent discussions. Yes, to answer you, I do find it confining. Imagine being the wife of a calvary officer, and your husband is gone for weeks at a time, months at the time, and you are here. Living among the enemy. When I leave this house, I am never certain how I will be received in the wider world. People seem to know I am a northerner, maybe my dress." She smiled at Meredith while brushing the front of her pale rust dress. *"Maybe we are not as much in the way of buttons, bows, and frills as the southern women."*

They enjoyed each other's company. Major Lovett was seldom home, and the children were well-mannered and a joy to be around. Three-year-old Rose and five-year-old Elijah, became Meredith's delight, compared to the rough and tumble townies she had taught. Playtime restored her assurance that she did really love children, although teaching had not been her calling. In fact, this search for her brother had a great deal to do with her calling as a writer. She was given an opportunity to travel and see new things and make inquiries. She read the children Robinson Crusoe and told them her own adventure stories too. Outdoors she taught them hopscotch, and they practiced tossing bean bags into a basket. The children had talent in drawing pictures. It reminded Meredith of Liam as a boy. The Lovett children often did funny pictures of each other and of Meredith, and they enjoyed and laughed at the results.

For Meredith, it was very much a diversion and respite from everything else. Certainly, a welcome relief from the loneliness that had been overtaking her. She was missing everyone, her family, her dear brothers, and sisters. The twins, little Percy and Cecil, were growing up, and she hardly knew them. Sarah was almost nine and never the same since the lightning. She missed Clarissa Clark and even Richard, a pain though he could be. Even her mother and, indeed, more than ever, maybe more than anyone: her father.

Meredith's life took on a new routine. Mornings with Martha, afternoons with the children, evenings writing in her comfortable room. Her despair would come and go, roll over her like a great wave. Yet Meredith looked forward to her days. The most troubling aspect was the continued deterioration of Martha, who now began to shake without a taste of spirits. By then, the two women had formed a bond. An alliance containing many facets; recrimination, guilt, naivete, regret, tears, and even a little laughter. When Martha told her things that were shocking; Meredith did her best to hide her reaction whatever it might be. After all, a virgin from the backwoods of Cumberland County, Nova Scotia hearing the intimate details of a Nashville public woman, who sometimes rambled on in an offhanded fashion about her dealings with men, carried plenty of shocking details.

"I have swallowed men's discharge. Oh yes, I have, yes sirree. I have licked the big pole."

Do such things happen, Meredith had her head down intently writing while wondering if men and women actually practice such perversion? Is this part of a relationship? Part of the marriage bed? I shall never marry, never, if that is what is expected of me. Some mornings, Martha was intoxicated and argumentative; some days so quiet she had to be primed with probing questions. Some mornings she was simply too sick, and there were no questions at all, just growing concern from Meredith, who was developing a bleak understanding of this woman. When she was feisty Martha would just let loose. *"I've even let the few that wants, lick my cunny. I hate it. It tickles. But it ain't love, don't think it is love because it has nothin' to do with love, even though some of them says it is."*

Three weeks passed, and winter held. It didn't have the bite of a Nova Scotia winter, but there was a nip in the air that made you haul up your collar. Meredith and Martha moved indoors to a tearoom and ignored the harsh stares of the proprietor, unhappy a public lady was gracing his premises.

Then, another letter from home. Meredith trembled when she saw the writing. It was from her father.

My darling daughter,

I pray for you every day and ask God to keep you safe. I am writing without Vena knowing it. I fear she is losing her mind. She has gone on something terrible of late. Her rages are taking over her body as if the devil was living inside her. I know she deeply regrets the manner in which she treated Liam and yourself. She drove Liam away and has ordered you to undertake this dangerous journey. We have your letter that you believe he is alive. Your mother wants you to find him and bring him home, but I fear that is impossible. Give it up, my dear. You have done enough, interrupted your life enough. Your mother asks too much. There is much sadness here too because your sister Janet has been jilted. The young man courting her has stopped his visiting, and I fear Janet is heartbroken.

There is some relief, however. Jacob has come home to us as the girl he ran off with was taken back roughly by her parents. They gave my boy a good thrashing too, and he returned to us black and blue and humble. His return has calmed your mother to some extent. She sometimes calls Jacob, Liam as if she thinks one son is the other. I do not believe you can find Liam, and I feel my dream of both of you returning to us can never be realized. I know you and Liam want to make your own way in the world, but to have you both here at home, one last time, even for a short stay, might bring us peace again. Do you remember what peace was like before poor little Flora was taken up to heaven? Despite my poor health, I still work hard. We have had good crops this year, and the neighbors helped us out some until your mother accused them of stealing cabbage and drove them off.

Life is hard right now, but Jacob is a strong hand. If you possibly could bring Liam home and yourself with him. It is the only thing that will give your mother rest, but you have done all you can. I do not expect to see you both back here, although I long for it.

Your father with affection and love,

Clifton

The respite of the past few weeks disappeared. Meredith sunk into a depression. She re-read her father's confusing letter. Give it up. My dear, you have done enough --bring Liam home and stay awhile until we have peace again.

Peace again. When would that be? Her mother hadn't had peace since that dreadful day. The image of those hours stands strong in Meredith's mind. It could have happened yesterday instead of many years ago. She was almost nine at the time. Running in the rain. The dear little darlings, running in the rain.

"Is something wrong with you?" Martha asked. She was now the interviewer, Meredith felt the tables were turned, that Martha, ill and getting worse, was the strong one. Soon she would be confined to the hospital. Soon she would lose this friend too, as she had lost Pauline McKendrick and Regena Raymond and Lieutenant Thompson and yes, even Billy Hunter. They were all somewhere behind her.

Then a sudden blow upon arriving at the boarding house. Major Lovett was waiting for her. He was in full uniform with his cavalry sword strapped to his waist, standing straight and tall in the parlor; his expression was foreboding.

"You will not be looking after my children another moment. I want you out of this house within the hour."

Meredith knew why. She had been seen too many times with a public woman, and it had got back to the major. She asked the question anyway.

"Why?"

"Because you have been cavorting with whores that is why. Do you think I want you around my children, spreading germs from whores?"

"I have not been cavorting with anyone. I am interviewing a woman to write about her life. Dear lord sir, what are you suggesting?"

It was useless. Major Lovett raised his voice to such a level it brought his wife and children into the room. A horrible scene ensued, with both Meredith and the major losing their tempers. Little Elijah and Rose were crying, their mother too, while trying to mollify all of them. It was made worse that Rose clung to Meredith's leg, and she would not let go and would not be pacified.

The major roared to such an extent it made his wife recoil, and the children fled the parlor. Mrs. Lovett wept as Meredith put her things together. She was so very sorry, she understood what Meredith was doing, but her husband's word was final.

"He is the head of the household; I cannot disobey him."

Meredith held her head high and smiled pleasantly at the major's wife, whose tears would not stop. They held each other in a long embrace, and Meredith excused herself and left the house. Upon leaving, she looked around for the children, but they were not in sight.

Meredith was back on the crowded streets of Nashville, carrying her portmanteau with her rucksack and bedroll slung over her shoulder, and her straw hat fitted firmly on her head. She was jostled by soldiers and civilians but too numb inside to give a damn. If she were run over by a donkey cart or a carriage full of carpetbaggers, what was the difference. She was exactly where she had been when she met Martha. Meredith realized for the first time the difficulty in being a journalist and trying to be anything else. There was the consideration of where to go, but really her only choice was to go back to that notorious hotel wedged to the Silver Dollar saloon and a whorehouse. The hotel with the smell of vomit and tobacco and the broken front door. She was disgusted by the thought of it.

Suddenly, out of nowhere, a man was at her elbow, grasping her arm. She wrenched herself free without looking at him. It had happened before by drunks on the street. He grabbed her arm again, and she was about to land him a good hard slap when he sang out in that very distinct drawl, that huckleberry voice. *"Hello, my dear."*

Meredith froze. Could it be? The bearded stranger smiled at her. It was Billy. He was suddenly holding her up, steadying her again, just as he did when she first noticed his wooden foot. Now Meredith was staring at the foot to confirm that it was indeed Billy Hunter. He was dirty, dusty, and ragged, his face hidden in thick hair. His beard was untamed and shaggy with streaks of gray. It certainly changed his appearance, but that smile was all Billy.

"Billy! Where have you been?"

"My dear, I was like Jesus in the wilderness for forty days. I've had the time of it, believe me. I was chased down by both Confederates and Union. The confederates heard me talk and believed I was one of them. The union boys saw my honorable discharge papers and let me go. So I got along with both sides, giving me what grub they could spare, which weren't much for them confederates. One of Chandler's wolfhounds almost got me. I had to jump in the river and stay there half a day until them dogs went away. Almost mauled by a bear once. I hauled up a couple of times to work for grub, but I tell ya, I am so very glad to see you. Where's that potter fellow? I know I didn't kill him. You with him still?"

"No, Billy, I'm not with him, and I'm leaving Nashville. My brother isn't here."

"I'm goin' with ya."

"You best not do that if they're looking for you. I'm going to try and stay clear of the fighting because the Union forces are digging in around the city, expecting an attack. But if you're wanted for the stabbing...."

He waved her comments away and told her nobody was looking for him. *"What's a stabbing with so much blood being spilled? Chandler ain't around here. Besides, the law is looking' for half the men in the county, nothin' to fear now. We'd be a respectable couple traveling again."*

Meredith was troubled with that idea. She was glad Billy was alive, but she knew what traveling with Billy was like. *"If you want, I'll pay for a bath for you,"* Meredith said.

Billy laughed, *"I know, I reek like an ole polecat. It might be the dried blood on this here jacket or the grease on these sailor pants. I am attired like them, free men working on the docks. I got money, but thanks anyway. I'll get cleaned up."*

The first chance he got, he ducked into an alley and stole a pair of pants off a clothesline. A few months earlier, Meredith would have been appalled at such action. She had seen a lot of things, and such observation had hardened her. Billy's action bothered her not a whit. She left him in the city center, agreeing to meet later. She got a room at the cheap hotel. The next morning, she would say good-bye to Martha and move on.

In the morning, a young mulatto boy was standing where she and Martha always met by the butcher shop near the tearoom. *"Martha, ain't comin',"* he said. *"She been put back in the hospital and ain't gettin' out again. She said you would give me somthin' for tellen ya."*

Meredith's heart sank, even though she knew the time was coming. The fallen dove was more ill every day. Martha was dying. Maybe they had caught her trying to work, maybe not, but the army, in charge of everything, had finally taken her off the streets.

The whore's hospital had none of the clean white walls as where Meredith had recently been employed as the doctor's assistant. The dank hall was musty with peeling paint and walls marked by scraps and dents. The floors were gouged and blackened. There was the stink of burnt cabbage and urine. Finally, after once losing her way, Meredith stood beside the bed of her friend. Even in the past twenty-four hours, Martha was more wasted. There was nothing anyone could do. Martha had a number of things wrong with her, the orderly said, besides venereal disease. *"Her heart is shot,"* is how he put it.

"Bullshit. I'll be up and around in a few days, and we'll continue my story," Martha whispered so weakly a teary-eyed Meredith had to lean in close just to hear her words. There would be no more interviews with Martha. No more breakfasts in the tearoom or outside the drummer's tent. When she left, Meredith stooped and kissed Martha's forehead and whispered, thank you. The dove was already sleeping.

Chapter 10

The hotel where Meredith had decamped was next to the Silver Dollar Saloon. Both enterprises were owned by a man named Silverman. The hotel was as disreputable as any establishment in Tennessee where men took women for money. They would take their liquor at the saloon and take their pleasure next door because it was cheaper than the brothel. In the daytime, the rowdiness of night was lessened, as if even sin had to take time off to rest. Meredith wrote in her room for three hours. She completed the story of Martha and sent it off to the Clarks in Portland, making sure it was addressed to Clarissa. It was not a happy story. If published, the good church ladies of New England would say a fervent prayer for Martha. Meredith hoped so. Her story, she felt, was in many respects a prayer itself.

Late in the afternoon, when she came to the little cafe where they agreed to meet, Billy had transformed himself. He wore a new suit, had a haircut, had cut his beard, and shaved. He smiled at her as if heaven had opened up and his Goddess was once more before him. That was the problem, wasn't it? His feelings towards her. Maybe she had cultivated it, had even encouraged it. Meredith hoped not, but she wasn't certain. But traveling with Billy was out of the question. The night of the stabbing came back to her. The sight of the flashing blade caught for a split second in the firelight, the splattering blood on her. Billy could not go with her. It would happen again. She would have to leave Billy behind.

Meredith knew she would have to deceive him, and it made her heartsick. Billy escorted her back to the hotel, they agreed to meet in the morning, and Billy scooted down an alley and disappeared. Where he went, she didn't know.

Meredith had her own plan: to take the early train to Memphis. And Billy would be left waiting for her at the station. It was a rotten thing to do, and she hated being so duplicitous, but maybe it would save someone's life. Her plan almost worked. But two minutes before the early train pulled out of the Nashville station, Billy plunked himself down beside her.

"Ya didn't think you was goin' to get rid of me that easy did ya?"

"I don't want to be with you, Billy. If you are wanted by the law, I'll be arrested as your accomplice. I'm on a mission, and it doesn't include being arrested because I'm with a wanted man.

Once more, he waved away such nonsense coming from a silly girl, but she would not let him.

"I don't think you understand the seriousness of my situation. Mr. Chandler already knows I led him astray the night you knifed the potter. If we run into him again."

"I did not know you led him astray. Thank you for that. You might have saved my life and we ain't goin' run into him." She stopped him with an abrupt question.

"Where did you get the money for the new suit, the new hat, the money you've got in your pocket, the money for the train? Where did that money come from?"

"I stole it. Hell Meredith. It's war. Everybody's stealing. All over the countryside, there are vacated confederate houses. It ain't really stealing if you walk through an empty house and take what you want. Spoils of war. It ain't theft if you stick-up a carpetbagger and take a few dollars off him."

"So, you are a thief."

"It's war, Meredith, don't you understand that. The rebels steal from us, we steal from them. The army steals from the farmer, and the farmer steals from the merchant. The banks steal from everybody."

"You're using war as an excuse, using the chaos as a vindication. Billy I'm very sorry I asked you to accompany me back in Falmouth. It was a mistake. You should go to Washington and get your military pension and find a nice girl and settle down somewhere. You cannot come with me. I don't need you, and I don't want you. You are dangerous. Mr. McCarthy will have a scar for the rest of his life."

He gave her a quizzical look, a half-smile, but his eyes were sad. The train was moving. Billy wasn't. He remained in his seat, staring out the window at the thriving occupied city they were leaving. *"We'll part company at Memphis,"* she declared. He said nothing, just slowly nodded.

"I'm sorry, Billy, sorry for ever getting you involved with me."

"Best thing that ever happened to me," he softly whispered without taking his eyes off the passing streets of Nashville.

Chapter 11

Their train passed the Davidson County line into open fields and gently sloping farmland. Still, here in the open country, the remains of war were evident. Did the Yankees have to blow up everything, she wondered. Only the brick chimney remained where once there had been a mansion. Beautiful landscapes, Meredith wrote, but so much destruction. Was Billy thinking the same thing? His eyes were glued to the window as if he were in a trance.

Suddenly the train jolted violently, the passengers bracing themselves as the brakes squealed in protest. The train slowed down to a complete stop. Billy went to the front of the car and stepped onto the platform.

"Soldiers," he said, coming back. *"Confederate artillery by the looks of it. Got heavy cannon crossing the track ahead of us. There's a lot of them."*

They waited an hour, sometimes getting up to watch the long gray procession as it moved north across the tracks towards Nashville. The Confederate offensive was about to begin. Off in the distance, somewhere, they could hear the muffled sounds of explosions. The train lurched, stopped, and lurched again. They were moving backward. The conductor came into their car, *"Sorry folks, we're going back to Nashville."*

"No." Meredith jumped out of her seat. *"Why, why are we going back?"*

"No choice," the conductor was already moving down the car away from her. *"They're blowing up the tracks; we can't get through,"* he said with resignation.

"Meredith, where you goin'?" She had her portmanteau, satchel, and bedroll and was off the slow-moving train, jumping from the platform onto the grassy shoulder of the track. Billy followed, clumsier because of his foot. He fell harder, knocking the wind out of him. She had hoped he would remain on board but knew deep down she

was glad he didn't. Still sitting by the tracks and breathing hard, they watched the train move backward away until its smoky stack was a speck. It rounded a corner and was gone. Thousands of soldiers, horses, and field guns were half a mile down the track moving in a solid line. She didn't realize how vast it all was, how many men, horses, mules, and cannon, were in a moving army.

"Why did you do that?" Billy asked. He was breathing hard and had not landed properly on his wooden foot.

"Billy, you should have stayed on the train. I'm going to Memphis," Meredith said, getting up and brushing off her coat. *"The train might take days or weeks. I am suddenly in a hurry to finish this mission."* Then like an old seafarer, she looked at the sky. *"You still got your compass? I figure south is that way."* His compass confirmed the assumption was correct. But the Confederate army was in their way. Thousands of men marching to the beat of regimental drummers.

"That's General Hood, them damn rebels is trying to take back Nashville," Billy said it had been the talk of the city. The answer to confederate prayers. Liberation. The offensive on Nashville was beginning. To avoid the troops, they lit out across open fields to make their way around the army. Meredith knew it was a mistake to leave the train. Her sudden lack of patience was getting the best of her. She was headstrong, even when she tried not to be. At least, small comfort maybe, but Billy was by her side, and yes, she was glad to have his company. Dear God, she was confused about him. One minute wanting to shed him as a snake sheds its skin, the next welcoming his friendship. Except in Billy's case, it wasn't friendship, but much more.

They walked all day, finally managed to skirt the marching army. The terrain was rough, and they had to stop frequently for Billy to adjust the belt straps on his artificial foot.

Bedding down in a small grove of evergreens, Meredith brought out some bread and a bit of cheese which they shared. They slept in the chill of a Tennessee night under the stars. The night turned colder and Meredith, as she had done so many times, silently cursed herself and then her mother and finally her brother. It had become her nightly ritual, to silently condemn herself and them and then, in a fit of remorse and conscience, pray for them all: her family and finally herself.

At dawn, they warmed themselves by walking. Then a bit of luck. They came upon a farmer and his wagon coming back from the Nashville market. They got a ride and prepared to spend the night in his hayloft until the farm wife intervened, ordering Meredith to get in the house. It wasn't decent for a young woman to sleep with a man in a hayloft.

The third day was warmer, and Meredith and Billy left, having had a breakfast of oatmeal and apple sauce. They had directions and knew which road to take and where to turn off. Meredith forgot to ask them if they ever encountered a flaxen-haired boy who played the flute. She felt peculiar when she realized her omission and wondered if, after all those miles and many, many questions, she had silently, without realizing it, given up the search.

Three hours along a dusty road, they heard the low rumble of cannon fire. *"Wonder what they're blown' up now?"* Billy asked. By midday, it had turned hot. Riders approached; four men could be seen in the distance coming out of the dusty haze. As they drew closer, Meredith saw they did not wear uniforms. Many Confederate soldiers did not have uniforms, but something about these men told her they were not military. There was a certain feeling as they approached that put Meredith on edge. Billy, too, suddenly seemed tense. *"Militiamen maybe,"* Billy whispered, *"they ain't farmers."*

The riders came to a halt directly in front of them.

"Well now, what we got here?" The man on the horse was unwashed with many of his teeth missing which made his sneering grin all the more sinister. A Colt revolver was strapped to his waist; his shirt and hat were stained by the dust of the trail. *"Hello, young lady, you and your beau out for a morning stroll?"*

"Good morning, yes," Meredith said as she and Billy attempted to walk around them, but one of the riders moved his horse and blocked their path.

"Now, don't be running off so fast. We ain't seen too many young ladies lately, and we would like to talk a minute if your young man don't mind."

"Certainly, but we cannot help you much with directions as this territory is unfamiliar to us, except," she pointed behind her, *"Nashville is that way."*

"Oh, we ain't in any hurry to get to Nashville. We'll let General Hood have his way with them first, might go in after and pick through the rubble, though."

"We're in a hurry," Billy said, taking Meredith by the arm and moving her deliberately around the horseman.

"That's really unfriendly, mister. If a man wants to talk to the lady, you shouldn't interfere."

The rider moved his horse directly in front of Meredith and Billy again, and the others closed ranks, forming a semi-circle.

"A bit unfriendly, aren't you fellow. Maybe your mamma should have learned you some manners. Taught you when to talk and when to shut-up. How come a young man like yourself ain't fighten' for the cause?"

"I have been in the war. Why ain't you in uniform?"

The rider was taken aback by the curt question, which he ignored.

"Why ain't you up there with Hood attacking Nashville?"

"Please leave us be," Meredith said. She recognized the tenure of Billy's voice, and at that moment, she was more concerned about what Billy might do than the riders in front of them. Glaring at the intruders, Billy slowly unbuttoned his coat. His knife was sheathed in his belt. Meredith looked at the threatening men and then to Billy at her side. There was silence except for Meredith's whispered plea, *"Billy, please."*

The situation had taken on a very ominous tone. One of the riders asked Billy, *"What you going to do with that knife, sonny?"*

Billy spoke up. *"My name is not sonny, and it ain't none of your Goddamn business who I fought for or where we're goin. Now move those fleabag hags out of the way and let us pass."*

The cynical smiles disappeared from the intruders. The youngest one of the riders said, *"He a southerner boy I can tell by his talk."*

"That right, sonny? You a confederate?"

"I'd rather eat rabbit shit than fight for Jeff Davis."

The leader of the group gave Billy a violent glare. Slowly without another word, his hand moved to his revolver. As he withdrew the weapon, Billy threw his knife with deadly accuracy into the man's stomach. The rider grimaced and fired once as he fell. The bullet zinged between Meredith and Billy. All three remaining men started shooting at Billy, who quickly pushed Meredith aside before he wheeled, stumbled, and fell backward heavily on the ground.

Meredith sank to her knees beside him. Many of the bullets missed him but not all. Three found their mark. Two in the chest, and Billy was gasping, wild-eyed, attempting to raise himself. He looked at Meredith and smiled and died in her arms.

"Oh dear God, Billy, no, please, don't."

A rough hand had hold of her hair, so quickly yanking her to her feet it took her breath away. The horseman was racing across the field with Meredith suspended off the ground. She was held by her hair, her useless feet bumping into uneven clods of rough ground but hardly touching them. She was repeatedly bumping into the fast-moving horse. Twice she was kicked hard by the animal's front leg as it galloped across the open field. Meredith's face pressed hard into the horse's flank. The close contact with a moving animal, the odor of steamy horse flesh, the pain in her head, and the deep sorrow of Billy lying bloody on the road. She fainted as her head was on fire. She didn't remember the rider going into a cluster of pines or being dropped unceremoniously on the ground like a sack of rocks. She heard her clothing being ripped from her body. Her limbs were paralyzed. When she tried to see what was happening, her assailant punched her violently in the face.

"That was my Goddamn brother, your boyfriend knifed." The painful blow had little impact; she was barely conscious but could hear something, more ripping: her undergarments. She sensed he was on his knees, undoing his trousers.

"Oh God, no," she whimpered. He dropped down on top of her as if a mountain had landed, expelling the breath from her lungs. There was fumbling and then great searing pain between her legs. Half conscious, she was aware the other riders had arrived. The man finished and got up and spit on her. There was talk, but she could not distinguish words, just sounds. Then another man was on top of her, and she lost total consciousness.

Meredith drifted in and out for the following hours, trying to open her eyes, but her vision failed to focus. She would awake and pass out and could feel the casual drying of her blood casting a crust on her skin. It was impossible to know how long she had been on the ground like a broken toy. When her eyes would finally begin to adjust, she believed she was dead because there was the feel of a different wetness applied by a caring and gentle hand. Was she being prepared for delivery into heaven? Had she been murdered or bled to death? Then, the soft humming, a musical sound.

108

Yes, an angel. She could see its form, hovering over her, a gentle sway with a melodious hymn, so softly sung it was hardly more than a whisper. In her critical state, Meredith was certain she had been received by God. She was in heaven. The angel was administrating to her. Ever so gently washing Meredith's face. Unlike her blood, this substance was cool. Nineteen-year-old Meredith McBurnie lying on her back in a copse of pine trees closed her eyes and surrendered herself, letting the angel do her work. When she regained consciousness, her first thought was if she were dead, why was her body throbbing so? Why was the pain so horribly absolute?

Meredith blinked several times, trying to focus, but her eyes would not willingly adjust. She opened her eyes sometime later and discovered that what she thought was an angel was a nymph softly washing her legs. The nymph was a young negro girl, no more of age than nine or ten.

"*Who are you?*" Meredith's voice was an utterance she didn't recognize.

"*My name is Chardonnay. You is hurt bad, but the bleeding down there has mostly stopped.*"

"*How long have you been here?*"

"*Been here the last day, maybe better.*"

"*Where are they, the men?*"

"*They gone, rode off after they did you.*"

Then Meredith wept. She convulsed, choking on her own tears. The young girl continued to softly clean her, working on her arms and hands. When she could speak again, Meredith asked her about Billy. "*They killed my friend back on the road there. Is he still there?*"

"*Nope, they hung him up, but the farmers cut him down and took him away. Them men that was here took the other dead one with them. They was going to kill you, but the younger one who didn't put his self on you he told them to leave be. I was watching from the trees. They didn't know I was watching.*"

"*Did you see them...ah, ... violate me?*"

"*I did but I could not help you until they was gone. I didn't have no gun. Well I did have a gun, but it only fires one bullet, and there was three of them.*"

"*How long. How long have I been here?*'

109

"I don't know, sun was high, now it's getting lower, three hour maybe. I fetched your bags. They went through them, but I don't think they took anything."

"My satchel, was it there?" Speaking made her hurt all over. She had never experienced such a blinding headache.

"You mean that book you write in, it's here. I brought everything here. There's a stream down there a few footsteps away; that's where I got the water to clean yous up."

Half an hour later, slowly, ever so slowly, Meredith tried to stand up. Eventually, with the young girls' assistance, she was on her feet, breathing unevenly and refusing to inspect her ripped clothing. Unsteadily, with her torn garments wrapped around her, Meredith and Chardonnay made their way to the small brook. Meredith craved water; her thirst was incredible. Her neck and face were covered in bites and scratches. The second man bit her deeply several times.

"Where can we get help and food, do you know?"

The girl shook her head.

"Where are your parents?"

"Dead, they was kilt."

"Where do you live?"

"Nowhere."

"Where are you going?"

"I don't know. Just going."

"Can we get to the nearest farm?"

"It's that way," the girl pointed. It took another hour, drinking and feeling cool water on her face, before she could move. Then, leaning heavily on the child, Meredith hobbled back across the field where she had been dragged. Along the way, she found the ribbon from her hair and then tufts of it. She wept openly in front of the child. She was ruined. Ruined and far away from home, her only friend had died in her arms. The brave, adventurous girl was gone out of her.

"The man with the wagon, the one who cut down your friend they hanged, he went up that road." Chardonnay said. *"I watched him."*

All Meredith could say was, *"thank you."* There was nothing else. Her long-held girlish dreams of sharing a virginal marriage bed with a man someday were gone. Something unspoken to others but highly cherished to herself. They hobbled along a narrow road as the sunset. A lantern came on in a farmhouse up a long, uneven lane where the heavy wagon wheels had cut deeply, leaving ruts filled with water. Meredith did not remember it raining recently.

A dog barked, a farm wife took over, and she did so with full authority. Chardonnay was told to scoot while lifting a crumpled Meredith in her ample arms and carried her off to bed.

"*No, please,*" Meredith weakly protested, "*I beg you, do not send her away. She has been so good to me.*"

The lady gave her a weak smile and nodded as if she understood.

"*I know, my dear, it is not in the Christian spirit to turn the needy away, but those free slaves are all over the place, stealing as much as Sherman's bummers. We can't have her type around here. We is poor.*"

Meredith began to tell her how Chardonnay had found her. The story was confusing, and she was asleep before she got far.

"*I was bleeding badly,*" were her last waking words.

"*I know, just let me tend you now.*"

There was nothing further. Meredith slept as the woman put hot bricks in her bed to stop the shaking. The farm wife administered salve on her patient's neck. She watched the growing swelling on Meredith's forehead and put a cool towel over it. She bathed the bruised ankles and feet. Finally, she covered Meredith in a quilt filled with goose feathers that she had made herself. The farm wife's name was Lucy Fitzpatrick. She did all these things lovingly as she did when her duty was called to be the matriarch of the Fitzpatrick clan. She kept watch over Meredith as her eldest daughters tiptoed in and out of the room, keeping the rest of the children at bay.

There was hot soup at some point. That was all.

The following days were a haze. She did remember that every one of the seven Fitzpatrick children came to inspect the patient. They were all interested in the curious woman from up north who was attacked by Yankee outlaws. The family was Irish. A large crucifix hung on the rough wooden wall above the bed Meredith shared with the two eldest daughters. The empty-headed Mary was crazy about knowing everything. Martha, her younger and prettier sibling was smarter. All the Fitzpatrick daughters were given Biblical names as a demonstration of faith in the blessing of God.

"So we can get into heaven. Only real Roman Catholics are going to heaven. Sorry, there are no Presbyterians."

She looked sorry, and Martha laughed. *"Are you St. Paul's little helper now Mary, declaring who gets in and who gets out?"*

"If you paid attention," Mary shot back, losing her prominence as older sister and not liking it.

After several days the sisters, particularly Mary, asked more questions of a personal nature. Martha was inquisitive also on every aspect of Meredith's attack and other things as well. Things she would not or could not ask in front of her sister. Finally, they talked about the war, and Meredith told them about the wagon train and what life was like in Nashville. Subjects in which they were keenly interested. Then just before going to sleep, Mary came out with it.

"Did they violate you? Mother will not tell me. That's what they did to Belinda Hastings. Yankees, many, many men violated her. More than twenty."

"Mary that's nonsense, Martha said. *"Belinda Hastings has never been violated. You believe those silly girls in the next farm. They stuff your head full of nonsense."*

Mary pouted, and Meredith did not answer the question. More than once, she would not answer questions she considered too personal or too horrid. After Mrs. Fitzpatrick got her up and walking around, helping in the kitchen with the others, Meredith would begin to see the world through the eyes of these Confederate daughters. They felt they had little prospect for a change in their meager fortunes. They whispered about the war, and they were uneasy. In the dead of night, with bed covers over their heads, they talked, and to Meredith's astonishment, they knew. These Fitzpatrick girls knew the war was lost. Living in a rural county, mostly away from people, isolated from newspapers and war talk, they understood the reality of things by the bare-boned news from their neighbors. Times would be tough for the south. There would be a price to pay. The Fitzpatricks' had already paid one price. Their livestock was run off by the United States Army. Meredith found their philosophy confusing. It was difficult to understand that this Confederate Christian family, pious in its ways, was too poor to own slaves but a family that believed in slavery. In all things, the Confederacy had been right and holy in its position. So, what was happening? What was God's message? To the Fitzpatrick family, all crimes committed anywhere in the south was retribution by the Yankees.

Chardonnay was never far away. After several attempts to run her off, Mrs. Fitzpatrick finally relented and let her visit Meredith.

"Where are you staying?"

"I'm out back," she whispered to Meredith. *"The mister lets me stay in the hayloft as long as his wife don't know. He gives me apples, so I is alright."*

Twelve days later, Meredith and Chardonnay were driven by farmer Colin Fitzpatrick to the nearest village with a bag of apples. Meredith had seldom seen the man of the house when she was helping in the kitchen and the during her final days at the farm, helping out with the milking. He reminded her of her own father. The same temperament too, Colin was quiet. The wives ran the families. Farmers have enough to do outside the house. Meredith had come to admire Lucy Fitzpatrick, maybe because she gave what her mother had not. Lucy had some funny ideas, and some of the things she said made Meredith cringe. But Lucy's comments were never directed at Meredith in a mean sort of way. She was kind and loving. There were none of the cold, critical words of her mother. None of Vena's chiding and criticisms; instead, there was compassion and understanding by a woman who cared for her as one of her own flock. She held Meredith's hand tightly while she told her what a fool she was.

"What are you doing out here with just that darkie? You need to go home where you belong. Next time you'll be murdered."

When it was time to leave them, no number of hugs or tears could tell the Fitzpatrick clan how profoundly thankful she was to them all. Words just didn't come to this budding writer.

The tracks had been repaired, and the train was sometimes running to Memphis. Thankfully the men hadn't discovered the money Meredith had pinned to her petticoat. The war was raging around Nashville. Farmer Fitzpatrick said the Confederacy was finished, and it was a damn shame as his wife was taking it hard. She had prayed so much for victory.

In her later years, Meredith would have few memories of the Fitzpatrick family or of Memphis either. It was another ramshackle town opening its arms to the commercial benefits of the Mississippi River. A town with strong Confederate leanings. She couldn't find a place to board that would consider taking Chardonnay even as a paying guest until Chardonnay herself suggested a place that had been kind to her. It was run by Mrs. Ingram, an aged negro lady, who showed refinement in her manner. She had been the housekeeper for the wealthy couple who hurriedly left the city, as the Yankee Navy let loose its first volley on the Mississippi River. Mrs. Ingram said the master of the house was highly placed in the Confederate government, so it was urgent he leave immediately which he did. Otherwise, he would serve out the war in a Union prison. The room was clean, and they had a real water closet down the hall.

Meredith was too heartbroken to write. She didn't pester the army about prisoners. The war was waging up in Nashville. She could care less. Most days, she stayed in bed attempting to mend herself. She had lost a lot of her dreams, ill-defined as they were. She always thought she would marry as a virgin. It was a great deal to lose. She had not only lost her virginity but her chastity, dignity, and self-respect. She no longer cared about finding Liam or writing stories for the magazine. The dreams she had brought to Maine, the dreams of a lifetime, were gone. Her imagination was as barren as a desert.

While her bruises were beginning to fade and a bit of power turned them into pale blotches, the deep sorrow within refused to dissipate. Mrs. Fitzpatrick's daughters had given her a scarf to conceal the bite marks on her neck and had mended her clothes as she slept. Meredith knew they had found her money and removed it to wash her garments, and they had put it back again. People who had little, had taken nothing from her and given much. Not a dollar was missing. Billy was wrong; everybody wasn't stealing.

When she began moving about, to her surprise, Meredith found that she encountered more courteous attention when Chardonnay accompanied her. It only dawned on her after a few days, that people took her as a woman of means who had managed to maintain one of her servant girls. After a week, she and Chardonnay took the train to Kansas City. *"Where are we goin?"* the nymph asked.

"I no longer really know. What did you say once, just going."

Chapter 12

What was Kansas City to her? Just another mud town. As the train rolled along the Missouri River, Meredith was unsure why she had come here or where she was going next. The assault had changed her. When she had left Maine and left the first and only employment she had ever really loved, Meredith was afraid she really hated her mother. Since the day when Billy died, she knew for certain she did. It bothered her tremendously. She prayed for repentance. It was evil to feel such a way towards the woman who had given you life. Or maybe it was herself she hated. Whatever it was, this was the end of the line. She had enough of being dragged through a war-torn countryside seeking the impossible. And Liam, what about dearest Liam? Was he damaged to the point he could not write his mother? What about his brothers who looked up to him? What about daddy, who was not well? What about "me," dear brother. Once we were so close, you confided your dreams to me. We shared them with each other.

"How dare you drag me through this. I want to slap your face. I am in Kansas City, and this is the end of the road."

She would find a suitable placement for the nymph. The child was a pet. Meredith had grown to love her. Maybe she could take her back to Maine. Because, damn it, she was certainly going back. Vena would not trap her. Never again. Meredith wandered the streets of Kansas City, Chardonnay by her side, never complaining. She asked for nothing, and Meredith was thankful for it because, frankly, she had nothing to give. When the war was over, and she was settled and established again in Portland, she would visit Lieutenant Thompson in Bath and tell him everything. Would he take in Chardonnay? Would she want him to? Meredith was in a walking daze. Once she walked in front of a speeding freight wagon, and Chardonnay pulled her back just in time.

They went to the Pacific Hotel, and Meredith got a room explaining her servant girl was with her, and no one seemed to care. Kansas City was big and crowded, full of Union soldiers. The Confederates had twice tried to take back the city and indeed had won battles on the outskirts of the community, but they could not dislodge the Federal troops from the town proper. The streets around Main and Delaware were ankle-deep in mud. Despite its grand parts, most of Kansas City was more disheveled than Memphis, but it was growing so rapidly. It was like a fat man who had pushed his suspenders to the breaking point.

Meredith was set on returning to Maine. She was planning the best route to get there as they passed a dry goods store on Main Street and Chardonnay went in to buy a penny jawbreaker. As Meredith waited outside, she read the notices and advertisements in the store window. There it was, staring back at her. It might just as well have been a daguerreotype of Liam. So strong was the cartoon of a farmer loading up his wagon with dry goods. The caption read - All you will ever need is right here. Tower's Dry Goods.

She staggered at the sight of it. Chardonnay coming out of the store, seeing Meredith weave, ran to her, concern on her pretty face. Meredith simply pointed at the drawing. *"That's him."*

When Liam made a cartoon, it was detailed in unique small touches, such as wrinkles around the knuckles that you would hardly notice. The ears were slightly enlarged and a reverted "v" line on his chin. His characters were life-like in most respects but carried those slight marks that Meredith described as his calling card. And there they were. The farmer loading his wagon with casks, bolts of cloth, bales of wires, pots, pans, and those hands of his and that face. The manner of his curved letters too. It wasn't signed by the artist, but it might just as well have been. Looking at it made Meredith feel faint. Chardonnay helped her to a bench in front of the store and went in to find the owner.

"My mistress would like a word with you," she heard the child say in a sophisticated manner, and Meredith wondered where that tone of voice came from.

An older man smelling of vanilla, wearing reading spectacles and a shiny pate, was standing before Meredith. He wore a long white apron that bore half the colors of the rainbow.

"Yes, mam, can I help you?"

"Excuse me, sir, but that poster in your window." She stood and pointed to Liam's work. *"Who drew that?"* He laughed at her question.

"One of the vagabonds drew that, a talented young fellow to be sure."

"Do you know him, know his name by any chance?"

"He was a fellow seeing the sights of the world and making his living with his graphite. Wish I could do something like that."

"Do you know his name?"

"Called himself Liam," the merchant said, watching her intently. Meredith could not speak. Dear God in Heaven! A needle in a haystack, and she had found the needle. She was breathing rapidly, as if someone was pressing on her chest. Chardonnay watched with wide eyes.

"Are you alright, Miss? I've got customers waiting, but if you need my assistance, well certainly."

"Just one thing, do you know where he is?"

"He said he was going to New Orleans and then possibly taking passage to San Francisco. Sorry, that's all I know."

"Just one last thing. When. When did he make that poster?"

"About two months ago. Sorry, I don't know anything else about him."

But it was more than she could have hoped for. More than she had obtained since beginning this search. Something sprung within her, a tremendous inner relief, like a pressure valve was letting loose of the force that had been building. Meredith took Chardonnay in her arms and hugged her. Chardonnay stood frozen, uncertain of what to do. She seemed to realize, although Meredith certainly didn't, the dangers of embracing a colored child in broad daylight on the streets of a Confederate town.

For the first time in weeks, Meredith felt optimistic. She wrote her mother that with the news that Liam was either in New Orleans or on his way to San Francisco. It didn't matter. At least he was alive.

117

That night in the hotel, with the nymph sleeping beside her, Meredith passed over her day, and the nagging questions returned. Why was her brother, a deserter from the federal army, and a wanted man using his own name? Why was he so seemingly unconcerned about being captured? Was there just too much water under the bridge, too far from Virginia to worry, too many deserters in the highways and byways? Was that it? Happily, she could now go back to Maine and resume her life. She hadn't found him, but it was close enough. The news would appease her mother. So, he was alive, and she had found him -- sort of. After a few days of contemplation, Meredith decided her best route back to Maine was to go south to New Orleans and get passage on a ship north. She certainly couldn't backtrack to Nashville; there was too much war around the city. She would take Chardonnay to New Orleans and take a ship to Maine. Maybe have a quick look around that city while waiting for a departure. In the morning, she would talk to Chardonnay and explain what she was doing, and if the girl wanted to accompany her to Maine, that would be fine. Her biggest concern was money. She was running very short of funds.

Chapter 13

Chardonnay had the biggest, most beautiful dark eyes that now settled upon Meredith across the breakfast table. *"You don't have to come if you don't want to."* "I wants to," the child said before Meredith had completed her sentence.

"It's, I want, not wants, remember we talked about language. Besides, at the dry goods store yesterday, when you went to fetch that merchant, you spoke like a lady. Where did you learn to speak like that?"

"From my mistress, I was trained to be a house servant. I never worked in the fields like my daddy and mamma. My mistress took me into the house early when I was little, and she taught me stuff like how to walk right and how to talk to white folks. Before that I used to forage and hunt with daddy whenever he was around. He taught me things too, that's how I kept alive."

She paused for a second, *"They is all dead now. Daddy and my mamma and the mistress and the house is gone, the fields is destroyed. Nothing is left."*

Who did that?" Meredith asked.

"Everybody, Bastard Sherman's bummers, the militias, the fevers. The first year of the war, nothing really changed for us except the master and his sons joined the Confederate army. Master, he was kilt right away. Don't know what happen to the sons. When Bastard Sherman came through Georgia, most of the slaves run off; some joined the United States Army. My mistress got the fevers. She died cursing that man twelve times a day, so Bastard Sherman he got good and cussed."

Meredith guessed Chardonnay was about nine or ten and was surprised when the child told her she was fourteen on her last birthday, which she had spent in the woods living on squirrels she had killed with her slingshot. Chardonnay followed the troops for a spell because big armies always leave stuff, and there were apples and peaches in the summer. Harder in the winter, but she stayed around the wood where she knew things her father had taught her.

"The house where I was a servant was burnt to the ground, but I knew the woods. When winter come, and it got cold, I started walking. Been doing that for six days when church people going north took me in their wagon, and I stayed with them until one of the men started taking an interest in me with his hands, and I was back in the woods again. Then I found you. I can speak better than you think, but, truth be told, white folks don't want black folks speaking like them. It makes them kind of funny, as if you are trying to be one of them."

"You need to go to school. Can you read and write?"

"Not too good but the mistress daughter Jane, she teach me a little. I'm better at reading than writing, and if I had the patience to practice every day, I would be able to read the big words. Jane always told me to sit still and don't fidget. I wasn't real good at sittin' still."

The slavers shot her father. They said for very good reason, that's how they put it to her. His brother buried him, and Chardonnay ran away just ahead of Sherman.

She didn't know what had happened to her mother. She was sold to another plantation in Louisiana. Later she heard her mother got the fevers and died. Chardonnay watched the mansion when it was set on fire. She had stayed in the woods near the house in case Miss Jane, the master's daughter came back for her.

"Would you like an opportunity for an education? To go to school?"

"Yes, but I have to make a living, don't I?"

"Eventually, I'm going back to Maine. Do you know where that is?"

"Yes, that is up north where they have wolves, and the wolves eat children, especially black children, cause we is sweeter meat." Meredith laughed, and Chardonnay smiled and said her father had told her that. Meredith said she hadn't seen any wolves so far and only once in Nova Scotia, where she was from.

"I would be pleased to see snow." Chardonnay said, and Meredith said she would see snow in Maine.

"I am running low on money," Meredith said, *"so we may have to stay put in New Orleans until I work for a bit and maybe sell a few articles and correspond with people."*

"I got money." The girl said, *"I sewed it into my dress just like you did, so I didn't lose it."*

Back at the Pacific Hotel, she handed Meredith a roll of bills. Not near worthless confederate bills but Union bills, the regular currency of the United States of America.

Meredith counted the bills twice. They totaled one-hundred dollars. Chardonnay was shy about where she got it, but finally, she told Meredith the truth under the questioning of a skilled interviewer. She took it off a dead officer whose body she discovered in a ditch outside of Mason's Gully. His horse was dead too, and the money was in the saddlebags.

"I got to live by my own wits. We always search bodies if they is officers for anything we can find. As long as the body is off by itself. My father say it's no good to the dead. They won't need it in paradise cause everything is free, so why leave it. There was this too." She reached under her dress, fumbled around a bit, and brought out a small, nickel-plated pistol with a bone handle.

"I thought about using it when those men were, you know when they were," she paused and looked at Meredith. *"But it only has one shot, and there was three of them and if I missed and."* Chardonnay suddenly began to cry aloud as if the memory of the assault and similar memories from other times came back to her. She had wanted to act bravely, but she had not done so, at least in her mind. Her tears were genuine and flowed freely from those captivating eyes. She was a very beautiful young women, or so she seemed at that moment. Had she changed instantly? Changed before Meredith's eyes, the child in her had fallen away as she flowered into womanhood. Meredith was speechless. She had been terribly concerned. Funds were low, and hotels were more expensive for a lady and maid, even if they did look a bit down on their luck. It was war, lots of people looked disheveled. Also, Chardonnay was growing, changing, and eating as an adult. With the sudden relief from that worry, there was now this outburst from Chardonnay; the last person who should feel guilty. She wasn't the one who impulsively jumped from a moving train and got Billy murdered and herself raped and left for dead. Chardonnay is my hero. The guilt is mine. The newfound funds and the sudden change in Chardonnay overwhelmed Meredith. Chardonnay needed her attention, and she turned to her with concern.

"I was scared. That's why I told you I didn't have a gun. That's why I didn't try. I was scared. I learned never to be scared, but I was, and I am sorry."

121

"Dear Chardonnay, there is no reason to cry. I would be dead if it was not for you. I die of shame when I think about it, but think about it, I must. The embarrassment and guilt belong only to me. Those men would have caught you and done the same to you and murdered both of us. I would rather have you here with me unharmed."

They went quiet for a long time sitting at the writing-table in their hotel room. Chardonnay wondered what Meredith thought of her and if she was worth keeping, and Meredith was stunned at what she now understood. Chardonnay trusted her and had put her life savings in Meredith's safekeeping to use as she saw fit. Had Chardonnay been uncertain before?

There was something else too — was life telling Meredith something? That she was not observant enough to be a writer. How did she miss so much? With Chardonnay next to her one week after another, how did Meredith not see her companion change? She ate like a horse because she was growing and developing. Next to her, day and night, and she missed it. Everything was suddenly shocking. She had not recovered and had somehow lost her equilibrium.

"You look sad," Chardonnay said. *"Are you sure it is OK for lying to you? Jesus don't like liars, and if I get caught lying in the mansion, I get whipped."*

Meredith needed to reassure her once again and wondered if she currently had the strength. She had to try; getting up, she crossed the table and pressed her hands on Chardonnay's shoulders, looking her directly in the eye.

"It was not your fault. You saved my life. My brother always took credit for it, but he didn't actually save anything. You did the right thing. You concealed yourself until it was safe, then you came to my aid. Neither one of us wanted it to happen, but I caused it. I did a foolish, foolish thing, impulsively I jumped off a train. I was a girl when I did that. When you found me in the pines, I was no longer a girl in soul or in body. It happened, and you witnessed it. It brought us together. It forged a bond between us. A strong bond."

Chardonnay watched and nodded and stood up and put her arms around Meredith in a strong embrace, whispering, *"I just wanted you to know I was sorry for you."*

They fell asleep in an embrace, fully clothed on the bed. They were weary. The day had taken all they had to give it. Confessions, newfound money, a bond of trust, and reliving past nightmares zaps the strength of the strongest.

In the morning, Meredith completed the long letter she had been writing to her mother. A letter of excellent news for her family. She imagined them in the kitchen, the joy on their faces in hearing her words, read by mother, in her chirping, birdlike tone. Even dour Janet might indulge in a smile. Certainly, Jacob would be wearing a broad grin, as would the twins. The relief would be considerable. Clifton would be delighted. Meredith imagined his big smile while listing and having his tea at the table. Liam was his oldest son, something both Meredith and Jacob, being the second and third children, understood the special status that bequeathed.

Chardonnay watched Meredith's hand flow over the page. She studied the curvature of the letters, the looping of the L's and C's and P's.

"You write nice. What is Nova Scotia like?"

"It's beautiful and British, but there are those who want it to be independent," Meredith replied.

"Is there going to be war?"

"I certainly hope not. There is disagreement about things, but I don't think there is going to be war."

"Why not?"

"Well," Meredith replied. *"maybe because there are fewer of us. We have to depend on each other. We are not a warlike people. Not that we haven't been involved in war. But it is not our way."*

She took Chardonnay's hand, *"If you want to use the money you retrieved from the dead cavalryman, we can go to New Orleans right away. I'll tell my mother to forward her letter to the main post office there. But of course, it is your money."*

"No," Chardonnay said, *"It's our money. We use it to go."*

It was a difficult trip that took them from Kansas City deeper into the wreckage of war in the Confederate south. The countryside was pockmarked with destruction. Railroad tracks were twisted; homes burnt and battered. Charred towns without wagons diverted for military use. They made their way from carriage to rail car as they hop-scotched into Meridian, Mississippi, then by some small conveyances to Harrisburg. At which point, there was finally an available train with a single passenger car that took them through the swampland to Baton Rouge.

They arrived in New Orleans at night, and the city opened up to them like a radiant pearl in the darkening sky. Meredith loved the place immediately. It had been occupied by the north for better than two years, but, occupied or free, it was unlike any place she had ever known. Its people were a vast array of races and cultures, strange languages floated along the street. Different languages and different sounds. Music came out of little alleys and made people want to dance. The spicy food, the way the ladies wore their satin, and the city's soft and distinctive murmur breathed new life into Meredith. Young Miss Chardonnay, dressed in her new Sunday-go-to-meeting clothes, and her lovely mistress fit into the city perfectly. For the first time since the assault, Meredith was alive. The great burden of this wretched mission was coming to an end. She would book passage for the two of them. If the ship wasn't leaving directly, she would have a last look around for Liam. But there was a new ambivalence about her. Finding him was not more possible and much less important than it had been a few months ago.

In the fine clothes they purchased in Harrisburg, Chardonnay looked nothing like the child in the woods and far more like the beautiful young lady she was becoming. Meredith supposed Chardonnay was a loving replacement for something missing in her life. Maybe a mother's love or the sister she had lost.

"*Maybe I can adopt you,*" Meredith said over dinner.

"*Would you do that? You would be my mother, and there is no more than a few years between us.*"

"*I know. They probably wouldn't let me.*" Chardonnay bowed her head.

"*It is better that I am just your friend.*" Meredith understood and said nothing. They ate in silence and an hour later began their last few days of a less diligent search for Liam.

"*Do you think we have much chance?*" Chardonnay asked as they left the hotel.

"*Well, all indications point to here. The man at the hardware store said Liam told him he was heading for New Orleans. What I cannot understand is why he is using his own name. Does he not realize he is wanted by the United States Army and the severe penalty for desertion? It's all very puzzling. But one thing is certain: here or not, you and I are going to Maine. This search is over in four days.*"

They used the only method they knew. They would examine every store and business window along the main streets of the city to see if there were any advertisements or posters they recognized. The logical place to start was busy Canal Street, crowded with vehicles of convenience for travel by the gentry, and freight wagons driven by burly men and pulled by strong draft horses. It was hot and steamy by mid-morning. They bumped into people, were forced to step around barrels and kegs and unlikely objects such as a grand piano being lifted by five men. There were horse carts and hand carts. The cries of fishmongers along with apple and melon sellers. Despite the congestion, they were tireless in their search, peering in every store window, sometimes getting in the way of people. Men tipped their hats to Meredith, and she smiled and ducked around them to examine the next window. It took hours. After Canal Street, they covered Jackson Square and the French Quarter. They returned to their hotel exhausted and flopped on their bed.

Just before falling asleep, Meredith whispered, *"I'm sorry for dragging you through this, but it's almost over. When I start searching, I can't seem to stop."*

After a moment, Chardonnay spoke. *"If I wasn't with you, I would not even be in this bed or in this fine hotel. Far as I am concerned, it is just fine being here with you."*

The next day they targeted Decatur Street and Lafayette Square. There was not much advertising or many posters away from the commercial districts. What posters they found were not by Liam. Once Meredith got excited for a moment, but it was not his work. She moved on. At the end of the second day, Meredith's feet hurt, and the old utter discouragement and frustration returned. That feeling that she wanted to throttle her brother. Why was it all up to her? Why was she the one who had to search? Why was it her responsibility? She had to give up the position she loved, when he was too unfeeling to write his family, too uncaring to inform people where he was. Damn him to hell. Then she prayed for him and for herself too.

Their hotel was near Lafayette Square. A rambling building with a huge sign announcing – NO COLOREDS – but since Chardonnay was considered the white lady's maid, it was acceptable. Sitting in the lobby the next morning, Meredith was waiting for Chardonnay and thumbing through the pages of The Daily Picayune. As she turned to page three, that long-lost needle in the haystack poked her again. Immediately, she knew it was Liam's work. There was a cartoon character pulling his mule out of a northern swamp. The exaggerated hands, the eyebrows, the little touches that her brother always incorporated in his creations. The masthead contained the paper's address, and they were out the door briskly walking to that location with the newspaper securely rolled up around Meredith's fingers. They walked at a goodly pace with purpose and determination, not noticing the carts and mules, soldiers and wagons or the gentlemen who tipped their hats or the ladies who ignored them. They crossed the bridge, vaguely recognizing the city was coming to life in the early morning trade. It didn't matter what the city was doing; Meredith was on a mission of grave importance.

They found the newspaper and stood silently across the street from the building. For two or three minutes, they stood there like statues in a park. People crossed the street, and people passed them by. Meredith held back; a new trepidation gripped her. She crossed the street slowly, Chardonnay close by her side as if she felt the strange vibration also.

Cavernous and hollow sounding, the noise of the downstairs offices filled the air with a low chatter. The odor of ink and tobacco and something stale hit them immediately. There were a dozen people making enough noise for sixty. Smoke curled in the air and lantern light shone through. Flies buzzed around the windows. A donkey was loudly braying from somewhere outside, and a mechanical slapping sound came down from the upper floors. No one paid them the slightest attention. Meredith scanned the room. There was no Liam. She approached a fat man with a red, sweaty face and inquired where she might find the person who drew the cartoon. The fat man had several pieces of paper in his hands that he appeared to be scanning at the same time. He didn't look up, just pointed, indicating they should go up the stairs. Meredith and Chardonnay quietly made their way to the second floor. The slapping sound of the printing press was still above them.

People nearby were holding a meeting. Meredith had some unidentified emotion. Was it a slight panic or the spine-tingling of a hunter closing in on its prey? They walked down a long hallway with threadbare carpets and walls adorned with paintings of former editors and past glories. Most of the offices were empty. In one, a large dog slept, raising its great head only to acknowledge their presence but made no attempt to get up. Despite the bright sunlight in the world outside, the hallway was dark. Then in the last office with the door wide open, bent over a desk, was the brother she had been looking for.

Chapter 14

Meredith and Chardonnay stood silently in the doorway. His fair skin and flaxen hair were darkened by the sun. The full beard made him older. He appeared rather unkempt, thin. They watched him for a full minute. It was Liam alright, so intent he could lock out the rest of the world. He had no inkling he was being watched.

Then that powerful undulation crashed through Meredith. It came in a huge wave of sorrow, love, and hate. She was filled with despair as she stood transfixed. How could feelings be so contradictory, so confusing? Meredith watched the brother she had loved a lifetime and detested more recently. The swirling memories of it all, the wagon train, Pauline, soft graves on the trail, the executed Irishman, the cursing wife, Billy's flashing knife, the potter, the doctor, the decrepit hotel, notes in steaming horseshit, pain, blood. Hers.

Gesturing to Chardonnay to make no noise, they turned and quietly descended the stairs and left the newspaper building.

"He is not your brother?" Chardonnay whispered as if they were still next to him. *"Yes, it is him."*

"Are you not going to speak to him to let him know we found him?" Chardonnay whispered again. Meredith shook her head. There was too much churning inside.

"I'll come back later. I just have to be by myself a bit first."

She sent Chardonnay back to the hotel to wait for her there. Meredith walked a long time with no purpose or direction. Her thoughts were running wild. She was feeling fear and didn't understand why. What was she afraid of? Afraid of herself, scared of what she might say or do to him with the hostility that roiled up in her. It was extremely maddening watching him sitting there without a care in the world, absorbed in his work and her subjecting herself to assault and attack.

"Goddamn him." The words flew out of her in the middle of a busy public sidewalk. Meredith looked around to see if people were watching. She had not meant to speak aloud. What was needed was someplace private, to be by herself and cry.

She wore a smart blue suit of silk, comprising of a skirt that touched the ground and a short jacket and bonnet. She was dressed better than many of the people she passed. Two hours later she was lost and had to ask for directions to the newspaper. She was still pondering how to approach him and how to keep her own emotions in check. What to say? "Mother sent me to find you," seemed so pathetically weak and stupid as if she had been instructed to go to the schoolyard to fetch a little brother. It was all so crazy. They had once been so close, even if, at times, Meredith had trouble understanding him. She wanted more than anything to practice patience but was uncertain how long her forbearance would last. Could all those months of turmoil over so many miles be dismissed? For some reason, Meredith remembered his embarrassing boast that always painted her as the poor victim who fell in the river and could not save herself.

They were nearing the end of their childhood. Meredith was already tall and stately at fourteen, Liam, on the cusp of manhood at sixteen. Meredith let him repeat the story. Never interrupting nor challenging his version of events, never arguing with him over it. He was so proud of saving her. But it was a lie, a childhood experience that remained vivid. It was a lie.

Clearly, the leader, Liam, had organized the children for a long hike. Vena was against it, but Clifton told them to go; he would look after things. They worked before daylight to get their chores done because they would be gone all day. They would march off the promontory and make the goodly trek into the valley below. It was a substantial walk, particularly for the twins Percy and Cecil. But the little ones had teased to be included in such a delightful adventure. Standing before his big brother little Percy pleaded his case for inclusion with such force and dignity Liam had to take them. What a troupe they made that day clomping out of the farmyard and heading down the promontory, trying to avoid the wagon ruts as they walked down the natural elevation known as Kirk Hill. Vena watched from the kitchen window. Meredith was the tallest in the group and the den mother. She already considered herself a fine lady and refused to carry the worms Liam had dug.

"If you want to be a fisherman."

"I don't want to be a fisherman; I just want to catch a fish. Give me something else to carry." There were moments of high excitement of the type children can produce, such as seeing a Kingfisher in a meadow or discovering a four-leaf clover. Children on a long trek often fall silent. They are more excited than they want to let on to the group, some of them knowing it was a special day and making a secret promise to remember it forever. Three hours later, with many stops along the way, they heard the river's continuous thunder that stilled birds and wildlife. The spring rains had been frequent, and the water faster than they had imagined. The spillage was spinning and collecting in whirling pools around both banks. There were wet rocks, some as big as dories, along both banks of the river. There was too much fast water to fish. They found a clearing in a pasture where they could lay their canvas on the ground and unwrap the smoked herring and egg sandwiches. The long walk had made them hungry. Meredith discovered a little pool deep enough maybe to try her hand at fishing. She cut an alder, ignoring Liam's advice that the water was too high and fast.

The novelty of their sister fishing soon wore off with the youngsters, and they looked for other adventures. Liam instructed them to remain in the clearing and not go near the river. Janet had her hands full watching Sarah, who already had wet feet. The roar of the river gave an added excitement to the day, and that's why the first frantic screams from Meredith went unnoticed. By the time Liam saw his sister, Meredith was being swept downstream. Without hesitation, he plunged into the water. Janet and the little one could hardly hear their own cries of distress. Sarah's wild sobbing was contagious with the little ones. The last they saw of Liam and Meredith was when they disappeared around a bend in the river: two heads bobbing in the rushing water.

Janet tried to contain her own fear, but the faces of the youngsters were chalk white. They ran and stumbled, trying to follow their older brother and sister, who had left them behind. Panic reigned. How would they even find their way home without Liam and Meredith? Terror had struck, and little hearts pounded. The adrenalin flowed through juvenile veins as they stumbled along the riverbank. But down river

Meredith's flowing hair was already clutched in Liam's hand. As Liam told the story many times, he had grabbed a low-hanging branch from a woodland shrub.

Liam was undoubtedly the man of the day. His brothers and sisters had not actually witnessed the heroic saving of their sister but in their excitement, they believed they had, and the story, verified by a number of eyewitnesses, got around. Except it was not the true story. Meredith was swimming with the current not against it and her feet had touched bottom by the time Liam clutched her hair. She was in shallow water and already safe. He must have known it too. They hurried back to their terrified siblings. Carrying the younger ones on their shoulders, they arrived at a farmhouse where they dried their clothes. The farmer took them home in his wagon.

Liam was a perfectly adorable brother, but Meredith despaired when he told the story of saving her life, which he always did at the worst possible moment. She never refuted his story, maybe because the younger ones told it too with such convincing wide eyes and wild, expressive words. So, it became a bit of a legend: Meredith almost drowned, and Liam saved her. She supposed all brothers and sisters have friction between them at times. But Liam was never so uncaring as he had been since he entered the army.

It was dusk, but Meredith kept walking without direction. Her head was suddenly swirling with memories such as the close times they shared in the glade, Liam playing the flute while she read. At times she would come upon him when he didn't know she was there. He was intense at his sketch pad or with his flute. A boy with a remarkable beauty about him. She had not noticed anything beautiful about the bearded man bent over his desk at The Daily Picayune. She would look for that particular beauty later when she was ready to meet him.

A three-word telegram was sent from the city of New Orleans, Louisiana to Vena McBurnie, Kirk Hill, County of Cumberland, Nova Scotia, care of the postmaster in Parrsboro. The telegram simply read, *"I found him."*

Chapter 15

After the telegram to her mother, Meredith still waited: uncertain of why she was suddenly hesitating in approaching her long-lost brother. The heat of the day was passing when she finally returned to the newspaper, but he was not there, and nobody knew where he was.

Meredith circled the same streets in the neighborhood, uncertain of what to do. Gentlemen tipped their hats to her; drovers didn't. Federal soldiers told her young ladies should not be walking alone and would she desire an escort? She did not take them seriously as noisy children were still playing in the dying light. Someone was making music with a squeezebox on a front step. Meredith was feeling very strange. Waiting until the morning to return to the newspaper seemed to be her only answer. After delaying their reunion for hours, Meredith had a strong and sudden impulse to talk to him. It was as if she had won a prize only to lose it. As she passed a rundown tavern, Meredith decided to look just in case. When she opened the door, the only thing noticeable was the cloud of smoke hanging over two dozen men leaning against the bar. Through the cigar smoke, she could see men working their jaws and frequently using the spittoons at their feet. She did not see Liam in the minute she had before a man in a white apron ordered her out, rudely informing her, *"Women are not permitted in here. This is a respectable establishment."*

"More's the pity," someone yelled, and there was laughter.

Meredith moved around the neighborhood. One street over, there was a larger and noisier establishment. She had noticed it her first trip around. Deciding for one more try before returning to the hotel, Meredith took a deep breath. There was laughter and music inside. She stepped aside and waited for departing patrons to move on. Another deep breath, and she pushed open the swinging door. There at a table directly in front of her, sat her brother engaged in uproarious conversation with two other men. Meredith's heartbeat wildly. The music and merriment had raised her temperature; suddenly, her blood was boiling. She had spent hours calming herself to approach Liam in an appropriate and civil manner. Calming herself was a total waste of time.

Meredith entered and stood directly in front of Liam's table. But he was so engaged in conversation he didn't notice her. One of his companions observed her initially. When Liam looked up, there was a split second of no recognition. Then his eyes widened into a full expression of shock. It was the stunned look of the truly amazed: mouth slightly agape, eyes fixed in perfect expressionless orbs. Then his face turned to stone. He managed to move his mouth, but no audible sound was forthcoming. The bartender was yelling- *"young lady, please, only women who work here."* He was politer than the man in the last establishment, but manners aside, Meredith did not move. One of the men at the table, with a slight chuckle asked Liam if this was his, *'little lady"*. Her presence stopped the conversation at nearby tables. Men in derby and straw hats stared at her in silence, suspecting she was a wife searching for a roaming husband: it would not be the first time. Liam slowly got to his feet. In a flat voice, he finally said her name, *"Meredith, for the love of God."*

He tepidly embraced her, but Meredith's arms were frozen at her sides. Patrons at nearby tables watched with interest. They suspected they were watching a different story: the re-uniting of a war-torn family. There was not a clink of a glass nor the thud of a wet projectile hitting a spittoon. The room was transfixed. It was war, after all, and the clientele had a certain respect for the importance of what they thought was happening.

Her brother took Meredith by the arm and walked her into the street. *"What are you doing here?* He was both laughing and crying, and she couldn't make out which was real.

"Well, Liam." Meredith wobbled slightly, taking an unsteady step towards him, uncertain if she was going to slap him or finally put her arms around him. She did neither. In a stone-cold voice, she simply stated, *"Liam, I have spent months looking for you from Virginia to Louisiana. Let me see now, I was weeks on a wagon train, where people were*

murdered, including a lady I greatly admired. Then my traveling companion, a young man, a veteran of the federal army was murdered, and I was dragged off by the hair of my head and almost murdered." Her fury was building, bubbling up inside. *"Goddamn it, Liam, mother sent me on this crazy chase. Why could you not let us know where you were and that you were safe?"*

Stiffly he made a half-turn as if he was about to leave her standing in the street. Then he turned and faced her with eyes she did not recognize. Something had changed in him. Her mind raced, trying to distinguish what was the difference. He turned away as if he could not look at her. She felt herself again slightly swaying while studying her brother's face that portrayed nothing. The surprise of seeing her had been replaced by resentment, she suspected, for being found. Meredith understood what she had considered many times in the past months. Liam did not want to be found. He wanted to be forgotten by those who loved him. In a voice she had never heard before, he said, *"You ask me why I did not notify you that I was safe? Because dear sister, I am never safe."*

He looked away from her, fixing on something across the street. He was older certainly, the assaults of life written on his face. He was thinner, the strong, rugged farm boy replaced with some unidentifiable change in his character. He had a hard edge to him, she thought, a trait not witnessed before. Maybe the scar on his forehead and the one under his left eye or the lines that had gathered at the corners of his eyes. Eyes that now looked wild in his wind-burned face.

Meredith could not distinguish or identify the unknown characteristics in him. There was undoubtedly pain and maybe shame too. The transformation was confusing. She had not expected such a different brother.

"You appeared very safe in the saloon with your friends."

"They are not my friends. I have no friends, nor do I want any."

Not knowing what to say, she said nothing. Whatever bitterness and hard feelings she had possessed melted away. She could feel her hostility dissipating as if it were perspiration drying in the wind. They went to a dining room somewhere. Meredith didn't remember where or if they ate anything. Liam drank some concoction; she had tea. The conversation was polite. He held back much until they left the dining room and went to a nearby park where, off by themselves, she began asking him the pertinent questions of why he had deserted them. Liam's answers were terse. He mostly declared he didn't know why he did what he did. There were no rational answers. Three drunks wandered into the park but left them alone. Another man came near, and Liam got to his feet. The stranger staggered away. There was something in Liam that seemed remarkably dangerous.

The joy of finding him was tempered by the mystery of who he had become. There was so much Meredith wanted to say. Yet, she knew whatever he had gone through had altered him. He was not the brother she remembered. The killing of that young soldier on a deserted road three years ago, that epic struggle with another young man: a dual without rules had damaged him. He had been involved in one great battle and survived yet he was wounded in a way that was more spiritual than physical. He was injured nonetheless. She tried to make him close to her.

"What are your plans Liam, where are you going?"

There were no plans; there was no destination. He was another one who was just moving: a few weeks in one place and on to another. The Daily Picayune hadn't offered him a full-time job, but they were buying his work at least, both cartoons and some designs. One of her first questions was why he had not changed his name.

"You are a deserter," she whispered, *"they are looking for you."*

He scoffed at her, as Billy had scoffed, at any suggestion of personal danger.

"Let them find me. The first days after I left the army, I walked in circles. It didn't matter where, north, south, east, west as long as it was away from those big guns. I didn't really care if they caught me. I don't really care now. Let them shoot me. I'm not cut out for fighting. To tell you the truth, I was rather drunk when I signed up in Boston."

"You drink alcohol now?"

"I do a lot of things now, Meredith. I've had to steal to survive, so I am a thief. I am a murderer and a deserter. I have robbed. I met other deserters and we robbed together. Once when I was alone outside St. Joe, I robbed an old lady. As she was handing over her money, she told me in that fine Missouri tone of voice that she was certain I was really a Christian young man who had lost his way, and she would pray for me. Have you any idea how low I was? I could have crawled away on my belly; I felt so low. I could not have felt more reduced if I had shot her. Believe me, I considered it. It was one of the few times I really felt anything."

He wanted news from home then was sorry he asked for it. It made him darker and more defensive. The bench they were occupying was by the park entrance and his eyes, reflected in the gas streetlight nearby, glinted a coal blackness.

"You know how abominable mother was to me. I wonder if any of you knew of my deserting the army. Maybe I was just killed on the battlefield, but mother would want some verification from the army. I never considered the army would send a telegram to Nova Scotia."

He took her hand, and she thought for a moment, he was the old Liam, the one she knew and loved.

"I hated mother when I left home. Yes, I admit it. I was still smarting by her harsh attention of me. I think of mother, and I get hot inside. It's like the other thing. Mother's face was before my eyes during that murder I wrote to you about. In dire panic, I saw her finger. Remembered, we called it, the accusing finger of guilt. When she jumped up from the table that final time in front of poor daddy and the youngsters and stuck her Goddamn finger in my face. It came back during the murder of the confederate. I saw her. It was her I stabbed."

He stood up and took a deep breath,

"Panic had overtaken me, I admit it. That lad, if he had just gone away, if he had just strolled away back to his camp, but he would not. We were circling each other, him with his knife, me with me kindling wood. I begged him to go. I told him he had an unfair advantage as I was unarmed. "Leave me be!" I yelled at him, but he would not. He kept talking of his ancestors and his promise. Then he had a chance to kill me, or at least I thought he had such a chance, but he did not rise to the opportunity. That made things even more dire as it came to my mind he was toying with me. Mother's crazy voice ringing in my ears, scolding me, watching me be a coward. Looking back at it now, that lad probably had things running through his head too and was just as scared as me."

Liam sat down again. *"I cannot think of mother without the image of that young Confederate jumping before my eyes. I would have written his mother apologizing for his murder, but I didn't."*

"It wasn't murder, Liam; you were at war."

"It was murder, Meredith. War is murder. They pretty it, but thousands of men and boys lying dead in the battlefield at Fredericksburg is something you don't forget. It's murder."

She could not convince him otherwise, and even discussing the subject made him angry.

Meredith told him everything she knew of news from home.

"Sarah is no better and never will be. The twins were almost teenagers, and Alice May Kirkpatrick was attending music school in Truro." Meredith told Liam about her position in Maine and the wagon train and her employment with the potter and the Hungarian doctor. Talking about her recent past was reliving it, and Meredith felt the weariness of the past months anew. She finally told Liam she must go, and he walked her back to the hotel, agreeing to meet in the morning. It was well past midnight, and the streets were quiet. The gas lights had been extinguished.

"Well, it looks better than where I live," he whistled. Perhaps seeing some conclusion to such a highly intense evening had refreshed his spirits. At the front door, Meredith turned to him. *"I have a traveling companion."*

He took a step back. *"Who is with you Meredith, why did you not tell me? You didn't bring mother?"* He suddenly seized her by the arms. *"Tell me, Meredith, you didn't."*

"Liam, let go of me. She is a young girl who came to my assistance when......"

Meredith cast her eyes on the ground as the great shame returned; the bitter sensation was back. It was nauseating that awful taste of bile and blood she remembered as if it were yesterday. That hateful thing could cause so much pain in so many places and force her to suddenly touch her hair. Liam watched his sister in the flickering lantern light of the Pacific Hotel's front door.

"She was a slave."

"A slave?" He looked at her with surprise, *"Meredith, they hang slaves. I have seen such things. A mob has no manners; it knows no bounds, pays no attention to the law. It just cries for blood."*

"They won't harm her. People think she is my maid. In many ways, it makes traveling easier. Apparently, the wealth of slave-owning opens doors for you in this part of the world."

Liam sighed; exhaustion swept them. There was no more they could take in or try to understand. It had been an incredible several hours. *"See you in the morning."*

"Eight o'clock sharp right here. You will meet Chardonnay."

"Chardonnay, that is her name?" He whistled again and walked away, his heels making a distinct sound on the sidewalk.

Meredith leaned against the front door and watched her brother until he was swallowed up in the darkness. She had found him but not found him. He was her brother but not the man she had been looking for.

Chapter 16

Chardonnay slept like an angel while Meredith tossed and turned and finally stepped to the window to look down on the street. She tried to imagine how to help him. The only assistance she could grasp was her solid companionship and understanding. She had to hold him close; help him even if she didn't understand him. Dear God in Heaven, she had hated him recently, trailing him through the states in rebellion. Yet amazingly, she had found him and had to support him in every way possible. Liam needed healing and to be reunited with his family. If not for her mother's sake, then for his sake, for the family's sake. There had to be a way.

When Chardonnay awoke, she found Meredith asleep in the chair by the window. The morning light bathed her face. Meredith opened her eyes when Chardonnay shook her with a trembling hand.

"I thought you was dead," Chardonnay said, *"I couldn't wake you."*

"I am fine, dear. I couldn't sleep. There is so much to think about."

"How is your brother?"

Meredith thought for a long moment. *"Different."*

Liam presented himself in the dining room precisely on time with important news. The war was over. The Confederacy had surrendered. Somewhere in Virginia, a peace treaty had been signed the day before. He had to hurry to the newspaper, they would have a busy day, and there would be work for him. The news had in some way rekindled him.

"Does it mean slaves will be free," asked Chardonnay.

"Yes, it does," replied Liam. *"But it doesn't mean white people will be happy about it. Particularly here in the south."*

It was the first time Meredith had seen her brother in daylight. He was extremely haggard, but with the hard eyes, she had witnessed last night. The eyes of a man who casts glances around him to detect advancing enemies. They were not the delicate eyes of a sensitive flute player and poet she remembered. He was rail-thin too, his coat shabby at the shoulders and cuffs, his trousers threadbare, his vest stained without a watch chain, his boots needed polish.

"He's very handsome." Chardonnay said when he was gone. It made Meredith smile.

"You should have seen him a few years ago," Meredith replied.

There was excitement outside, and they did not want to miss it. People were celebrating, some already drunk, excitedly shouting. Shotguns were fired in the air. The soldiers were particularly overjoyed. Seeing the end of military service and the sweet thoughts of returning home were suddenly overpowering. People were excited. There was back slapping and joyful salutation. Celebration was everywhere driven by soldiers, but plenty of local people joined in. The slave huts were empty. There was no one to work. Rich confederate families who had fled would now return to empty plantations. Meanwhile, faithful supporters of the Confederacy hid in their houses.

The festive mood was amplified by the fiddle, banjo, and accordion from hotel balconies. The most boisterous partying was carried on by soldiers, strangers, or transitory residents to New Orleans. But even here, in the deep south, Meredith felt the great relief of the citizenry. It was in the air. The streets were filled with those celebrating. Bonfires in the middle of the afternoon were built by men in blue uniforms. That night the city was a rollicking party. Meredith took in the sights and sounds and wrote a fine story for Portland. A firsthand account of the day New Orleans heard the news.

They did not see Liam until late the next afternoon. As Meredith sat with Chardonnay over a steaming pot of coffee, Liam joined them with a brisk, *"Good afternoon."* Before sitting down, he was most charming to Chardonnay, who was flattered by his attention. Meredith gave herself a mental note to talk to her very soon.

Then he turned to Meredith, *"If your sole mission, as you say, was to find me. Mission accomplished, what are your plans now?"*

"If we can secure a ship. I plan to leave right away. There are some northern ships along the docks, so there is hope."

"And this young lady, what of her."

"She is coming with me."

Then a moment of sudden inspiration. Meredith knew what it was; the issue she was struggling with, what she wanted to say. *"Unless you come with us. If so, we will go home to Nova Scotia. Would you consider that?"*

The look on his face was blank. Dear God, had she blundered? Had she made an irreversible mistake with him too soon?

"I think not," he said, *"although I would dearly love to see papa and the boys. But no. I shall refrain from that desire."*

There was, she thought, a certain hesitation in his response. There were good reasons he would want to go. The only person standing in his way was his mother, but then she was the major catalyst for everything. If she were not the driving force in our lives, we would not be here. Meredith had broached the subject, and she would work on him.

A month or so at home to smooth things over, she told herself; bring them all together again, and then he could go off to California, and she and Chardonnay would travel to Portland. It would work; she would make it work. She would have her father, Jacob, Sarah, Janet, and the twins on her side. Her mother was highly unpredictable. It was possible, with great patience, to mollify her at least to some degree. Vena could be placated for a day or two, then a blow-up, over anything. Clifton would try to calm her, but he did not have the words to do it. No one did really until Meredith took over the job as chief herder of the family, the one charged with keeping the reins on mother. Then, as Liam had done, Meredith left. *"Ran Away,"* Vena decried, *"to the Boston states."*

Reuniting everyone would be Meredith's gift to her family. Even if such a reunion were not totally successful, Meredith could live her life knowing she had done her best to reunite her fractured family.

Meredith, Liam, and Chardonnay walked the streets looking much like a respectable family out for a stroll; a returning soldier, his wife, and maid: nothing out of the ordinary. The man was more shabby and less prosperous than the ladies: but men everywhere had a similar appearance; ragged and haunted - returning from war. The contrast was unnoticeable in the city full of public women, soldiers, former soldiers, thieves, panhandlers, swindlers, and deserters. A fifth of the Confederate army had deserted, and the Union army did not care a whit: one less rebel to kill on the battlefield as Billy had said.

Liam took them to The Daily Picayune, where he demonstrated his ability by drawing a quick sketch of Chardonnay, who was delighted by his presentation. Liam had many jobs at the newspaper, apparently even running messages when necessary. There were occasional wages. The hundred thousand people of New Orleans had been under federal occupation for better than two years. The newspaper had been suppressed by the army governor for forty-four days for reporting too much about the glorious defeats of the federal forces of the United States government. It had just re-opened, taking a more cautious editorial stance. Only those who loved newspaper work remained.

Liam took his sister and Chardonnay to his other place of occasional employment - the docks, where he supplemented his meager newspaper income unloading Union ships. Meredith watched for vessels flying the flag of Nova Scotia. Most sails were furled, and no flags were in evidence.

"I have to leave you now. I may get a bit of work here today," Liam said, gently touching his sister's shoulder and bidding them good-bye. From a distance, they watched him striding along the crowded docks to stand in line with other rough-looking men. Every time they said good-bye, the same chill came over Meredith, a secret fear she would never see him again. He had made no promise to meet later, and Meredith suddenly felt so very insecure, knowing it would be easy for him to just up and disappear. Meredith shook off such nonsense; there were immediate considerations. She must be judicious with the funds Chardonnay had provided. They must seek passage north with or without Liam. She had demonstrated her love for him, but if he had decided to jump a train and flee, there was nothing more to be

done. If Liam fled, then there was no hope for a reunited family. Everything would be for nothing. It was all up to him.

"Why are you crying?" Chardonnay asked, getting into bed that night. The concern in her tender voice was always a balm to Meredith. She told herself what happened in the future; her mission had not been a waste. It had brought this loving girl into her life. Her words and embrace soothed a troubled soul. It finally permitted Meredith to sleep. But her sleep was anything but peaceful. She had the same reoccurring dream of that day years ago when she was ten years old, and all the world's heartbreak swelled up in her young heart. It was the time that made the bond between brother and sister very special.

The rain was authentic in her dream: that's how it always began. Her young sisters, Flora and Sarah, had taken a bucket from the barn to collect wild berries in the meadow just beyond the farm. Meredith was putting out the washing and watched the little girls running and laughing, holding the big bucket between them.

They had been in the fields no more than twenty minutes when the first drops fell without warning. Great black clouds rolled over the horizon, and the light rain quickly snarled itself into a thundering storm. Meredith ran to get her washing. The girls were tiny objects off in the distance. They had started running for home in the deluge. They could hardly be seen in the unleashed torrent. A year older than her sister, Flora was holding the bucket and was slightly ahead but still clutching her younger sister's hand.

"Oh dear God in Heaven, they will be soaked," someone said, coming to the front door. The rain rapped on the roof, beating down and dancing in defiant splashes in the barnyard. Thunder roared as if a great ship was firing its cannons, and the heavy balls were rolling across the sky. The thunder seemed to shake the earth. Liam raced across the fields, ready to clutch his little sisters and carry them swiftly home. Suddenly the black sky was full of streaks of fire. The little girls kept running but slower, now their tiny legs tiring, and it was all open meadow and nowhere to take shelter. Those two little darlings running in the rain would stay with Meredith forever.

She awoke covered in sweat; Chardonnay was shaking her. *"You crying out loud and rocking the bed. What is wrong, Miss Meredith? You having a very bad dream, worst I've ever seen you have."* Meredith put her back to the headboard and wept in her hands.

Chardonnay embraced her. *"What is wrong that makes you so unhappy. You found your brother, that should make you feel good but you crying. Why?"*

Through sobs and tears, Meredith related the terrifying flash of lightning that struck her little sisters. That terrible illumination. The hidden fist of fire that raised their petite bodies into the air and bounced them off the ground as if they were rag dolls thrown in an adolescent temper tantrum. It was an awful, gut-wrenching sight to witness. The girls flopped to earth. Still a hundred paces from them, Liam was followed by his father and other family members running from the house. The entire McBurnie clan was running in the rain, and Vena was screaming at the lightning. When Liam reached the girls, smoke was coming from little Flora's ears. Liam sank down beside the children and clutched them both. Sarah was moaning. Clifton, winded, sank down and took Flora from his son.

Everything stopped at the McBurnie farm: Little Sarah was taken up to bed. She was breathing, at least. Jacob galloped off to get the doctor. Flora was laid out on the parlor table. No one had to say it. Everyone knew the beautiful golden-headed child was dead.

Vena did not scream or issue a verbal complaint but trembled instead, biting her bottom lip until streaks of blood ran down her chin. She stayed with the living child and held Sarah's hand throughout the night. Even when the doctor arrived, she would not let go. They all fervently prayed for her. Sarah regained consciousness and mumbled a few words. The doctor said she would survive, and they would have to see what damage was done. The next morning as the first rays of the new sun streaked across the farmyard, Vena raised herself from a sleepless night and went to the parlor to gaze upon her other dear daughter: the most beautiful of all her children. The ladies from nearby farms had fixed Flora's body and put her in her Sunday garments. They brushed the child's golden hair and dressed her in white. If ever a child resembled a white angel, it was darling little Flora. Meredith and her mother cried together, for truly their hearts were broken. Baby Julia had died the previous year from the croup, but that had been expected as the child had lingered for several days, giving them some time to prepare. They had some warning.

Chardonnay listened without a word, but tears streamed down her cheeks, too, as she felt the pain coming out of Meredith.

143

"That's why Liam and I are so close. The two of us found our own hideaway in the woods. A place just for us where we could go and talk and be alone with our thoughts. It made us more than just brother and sister. We became fast friends too. It was after Flora's death that Liam took up the flute. He used to go to the wooded glen near our farm, and I would hear him and join him there when I could. I would watch the stream and listen to him. It was our peaceful place: it made everything better. And now I see him and do not feel I know him. He has changed, but I cannot find exactly how he has become different. I see no peace in my brother now."

"He will get it back." Chardonnay said with the type of direct authority she displayed at times as if she had lived beyond her years.

"My father's name is Clifton. He built a cemetery at the edge of our farm, not far from where my sisters were struck down. My brothers Liam and Jacob dug the grave, and father built a picket fence around enough land to hold twenty graves. It was his intention we would all be buried there: near darling Flora."

"And your other sister, the one who lived?"

"Sarah has never been quite right since that time. She has never passed the age of five, although she is now fifteen."

Meredith rose and said no more. She did not share details of the funeral, although she remembered everything. The funeral of a small child is unlike any other ceremonial occasion. It is like looking through the wrong end of a spyglass. The pallbearers appear large, carrying a tiny coffin through the barnyard, along the vegetable garden, and into the new cemetery. Meredith had relived the scene a thousand times: the little white coffin carried by four men, led by a piper, on a slow, agonizing march of mourning. The family was followed by acquaintances, cousins from River Hebert, a few local dignitaries, a thin string of county people, and a few townies. Clifton walked behind the pallbearers. Vena behind him, resting heavily on Meredith's arm. Rain threatened but did not come. Vena stood straight and strong until the end of the service when the child was lowered into the ground, then she sobbed and withered into the considerable girth of a cousin.

"I must make Liam come with us. I need to take him home. Help me if you can. We must convince him."

They dressed and went for breakfast. Meredith was relieved to see Liam loitering outside the front door of the hotel. He had worked late, he said, because many of the stevedores were drunk, and the ship was not completely loaded until midnight. He had enough wages to buy them breakfast. *"It is only fair I pay something to match your generosity."*

They discussed finding a ship to take Meredith and Chardonnay north without mentioning anything about Liam accompanying them. He would make inquires at the newspaper, and they would meet in the mid-afternoon. So, the search for a northbound ship began in earnest. The army was of no help. Brisk young lieutenants, telling Meredith they were never sure about Nova Scotia and whose side Britain had been on; as a flourishing trade was conducted with the Confederacy and his majesty's government. However, on the third day of searching, Meredith saw the red banner with the Union Jack in the upper left corner. It was the flag of Nova Scotia.

The ship was the *Abbie Perkins*, a Bay of Fundy brig built in Wards Brook, less than twenty miles from Meredith's family home. They shared a locality with the captain, that wonderful connection of home that got Meredith and Chardonnay on board. The congenial captain knew Clifton and showed them his boots repaired at her father's cobbler shop.

"What are ya doin' way down here, Lass?"

"I've been writing about the war." He raised his eyebrows, *"Ah, Lassies are nursing too these days and teaching and getting out in the world. It's quite a different day."*

The captain explained that the ship was new and tightly built, but there were no sleeping quarters for ladies, except for swinging hammocks below deck, and it would not be comfortable. Her brother could work his passage as they were short on crew, and Captain Hatfield did not like the look of any of the scruff on the New Orleans waterfront. They were leaving within the week. Time, she hoped, to convince her brother to join them. Meredith considered that her dreadful dream of Flora just might be the answer.

Meredith left Chardonnay at the hotel to practice her reading. She wanted time alone with Liam. This would be a special meal, she thought, a celebration of sorts. She had found her brother and booked passage north, a Nova Scotia ship incredibly landing them almost at her parent's front door.

"Liam, I feel rather festive this evening. Let us order some sherry."

"You drink spirits, Meredith? I am greatly surprised."

"Well, it's not alcohol really; I mean, it's not like whiskey or something like that."

"You are so innocent in so many ways, my darling sister. It is exactly like whiskey, and it can get you rip-roaring drunk."

"Well, I'm going to have a glass anyway. I had sherry with friends in Virginia."

"You have friends in Virginia?"

"I do, army friends; they helped me. I will say they did much more than the federal army has done here or anywhere else."

They ordered seafood salads and talked but a few minutes before, Meredith said, *"I had a dream about Flora last night. It seemed very real."*

He said nothing but waited. *"The death of our little sister brought us together, made us more than brother and sister. To be frank, if Jacob had deserted the army, I do not think I would have undertaken the task of trying to locate him. But it was you, my dearest Liam. You and I grieved together, and it made our bond so very strong. So, I am going to ask you, and I hope with all my heart you will agree."*

"You want me to come with you, is that where this is leading?"

"Yes, I want you to come with us; let us be a reunited family. Stay only a month but leave on a high note. If mother is bad, I will admonish her. The last time, before you went off, I remained too quiet, too passive when mother was having her tirades. I will not remain silent again. She cannot cower me now, not after what I have been through for her. For you."

"No, no, not for me. You did it for mother. I did not want to be found, although I must say it is good to see you, something I never thought would happen."

"So, Liam, spend a month at the farm and then what, where will you go?"

"It is crazy, I would ever consider returning. But to answer your question. California, I guess, is my plan, as much as I have a plan."

"You have always wanted to go to California, fine go, but come home first. Think of father; think how it will boost his spirits to see you."

He looked at his right hand, moving his fingers back and forth. *"It was this hand I used to kill him. This is the hand that drove the knife into his chest."*

"We all have had difficult, violent experiences, Liam. You are not alone. I was dragged by the hair of my head into the woods and assaulted by several men. Raped Liam, I was raped repeatedly. The fact I am even telling you this demonstrates how desperately I want you to come home. Let father see you once more before he passes from us."

The waiter interrupted them, and Meredith picked up her fork, refusing to cast her eyes on her brother. She was highly embarrassed, belittled, and startled by her sudden confession. She had made a secret pledge never to reveal her assault to anyone - except Chardonnay, no one would ever know. Meredith had broken that pledge and made something worthless that had been so highly important. Revealing it made her feel so very strange, as if she no longer knew herself. When she finally raised her eyes, Liam had not touched his food but was staring at her. He had become very pale.

"I am sorry, Meredith. Were they caught, the men, who did that, were they caught?"

"No, and they won't be. Not for that, but maybe, if God is just, for something else."

"You have already booked passage for me, haven't you?"

"No, not exactly; Captain Hatfield will take you as crew if you present yourself in an able manner to him. He knows father and has been in papa's shop to have his boots repaired. It was just a fortunate stroke of luck that I found a Nova Scotia ship and a Nova Scotia ship that docks in Parrsboro."

"A sailor now is it. I have never been a sailor. Maybe I will take a liking to it."

"You have a week to adjust to it, to get ready."

"If I must go with you, I am ready now."

Chapter 17

The *Abbie Perkins* was small, only one-hundred and seven tons, but she was neat and tight, launched less than a year earlier, and once out of the doldrums of the Mississippi River, her full-rigged sails madly grabbed the wind, giving her remarkable speed. Meredith stood at the gunwales, fascinated as the coastline sped by. Captain Hatfield told her of his former ship that had made Halifax to Boston in three days, "and there were vessels done better than that." Meredith remembered the torturous ten to twelve miles a day on the wagon train. As long as they didn't hit the 'calms,' good winds could carry them to Nova Scotia in fifteen days, although it might usually be longer.

Liam spent his first days throwing up. He vomited on his trousers and once on the ropes when the crew was bringing the ship into the wind. Liam took the teasing well and made himself popular by sketching crew members in cartoonist characterizations. He gave them funny faces with exaggerated noses or ears. The captain's portrait he took more seriously: it was a remarkable likeness, a portraiture rather than a cartoon. Captain Hatfield was impressed; they could tell by his demeanor. He thanked Liam with a graceful bow and then hurried to his cabin to put his sketch in a safe place to show his family.

There were eight men on the crew, including the cook, who also took a turn at the wheel. By the third day, Liam had overcome his sickness. Meredith and Chardonnay remained remarkably healthy but spent as much time as possible on deck as the air below was humid and carried olfactory sensations of grain and molasses. Meredith watched Chardonnay and her brother laughing as he drew a new picture of her.

Chardonnay continued to transform herself into a young woman. In the months they had been together, she had grown taller and was developing in other womanly ways. Liam flattered her with a new picture of herself every day. Meredith knew her mother would be stewing at home over her lack of communication from her wayward daughter. In her last letter, Vena had new concerns. One major problem in her mother's mind was the United States. Once the war was over, Vena believed the U.S.A. would turn its guns around, attack Nova Scotia, and take all the British possessions to its north.

Meredith suspected her mother would give her trouble over Chardonnay. Vena had been ambiguous on the subject of slavery. She revealed to Meredith once that her Christian values told her slavery was wrong but, *"All them running free, dear me, I don't know."*

Without giving her too much information, Meredith would make her mother see that Chardonnay had saved her life. She would not be staying in the hayloft in the barn but in the house with the family. Vena would see the price her daughter had paid to bring Liam back, and Meredith would answer no more commands, pleadings, or summons from her mother. The line that needed to be drawn would be drawn quickly, within the first twenty-four hours of their homecoming. There would be no mistake about times or places or where and when she was departing for Portland. Liam would have to do the same. Nothing would be left to chance. All Meredith could do was this one last push for family unity. Her last, Hurrah!!

She watched her brother and her daughter - yes, that's what Chardonnay was to Meredith, a daughter gratefully accepted as solid collateral by the heart. The mate's whistle brought Liam to his feet and the crew were at the sails. The spell was broken, the wind was changing, and Meredith stood up looking at the sea. It was time to go below.

Too much time to think on an ocean voyage but much better than a wagon train. She smiled to herself. Her final hope rested on her mother. Meredith wished for the best, that her mother would accept Chardonnay as her brother had. That would be perfect.

Chapter 18

Little did Meredith know, or was she even slightly aware of the chemistry swirling around the couple she had been so recently admiring. Chardonnay had never met anyone like Liam. When Meredith first described him, there was this picture of him directly behind her eyes that Chardonnay could call up whenever she desired. Just as she could call up the face and words of her father, what little she saw of him. In Chardonnay's young, fanciful mind, Liam was old enough to be admired as a father and young enough, handsome enough, to be a husband too. Not a legal husband, certainly not, but many white men took black women. Chardonnay was not naive; like most young negro girls, she completely understood how life worked. Besides, had the master himself not told her mother once that white men cannot marry across the line. Chardonnay had heard him say it and knew he meant the colored line cause he had already crossed every other line. But she greatly admired Liam; he was fascinating company for her. She liked to listen to him talk, and he would play the flute sometimes when she asked him. He did lovely sketches of her and smiled at her. Chardonnay was not accustomed to spontaneous smiles or gifts. She loved his kindness. Oh, she could see the damage in him. It showed in his eyes as if his spirit was on fire. He was haunted, she reasoned. Plain as day.

For Liam, the girl gave him enjoyment free of family bonds, the very bonds he was heading for. The weight of it tied him up. When entertaining Chardonnay, that weight could almost be ignored. What a breath of spring she was. Her laugh alone was worth a bar of gold. The cynical might call it a girlish giggle, but it was so musical, it was better than any flute. Once they got to the farm, he wanted to take her to the glade by the stream. He would like to hear her laugh filtered through the swaying soft needles of the pines. He would sketch her by the pool below the little waterfall or maybe surrounded by the spruce. She impressed him too. So much knowledge for someone so young. They talked a great deal about foraging, a subject they knew well. Chardonnay was so good at it, better than him. She knew so many things that one could be sustained by in the wild. He would take her to his favorite place, play his flute for her, and listen to her laugh. That was the secret gift he gave himself to relieve the many cross currents and emotional forces running through him. He was not exactly aware of how sexually attractive she was becoming until that very afternoon when he felt his erection. Although she didn't let on, he understood Chardonnay had noticed it too. *"Dear God, am I crazy?"* He thought to himself. Inwardly, where he spent much of his time, he laughed at himself, almost in glee, and told himself he probably was crazy.

A ship has nooks and crannies, storage lockers, and little spaces to put things. If one wanted to conceal themselves, they certainly could, but it is best to carry on, if not a romance, a strong case of mutual admiration on deck where only the eagle-eye would catch the drift of things. When not standing watch, when not hauling rope, Liam was beside Chardonnay.   They carried on day after day when the weather was fair, and he was free for five minutes here and there, depending on the whim of the captain, the first mate, and the winds.

Meredith had not noticed because she had turned in on herself. She needed time with her own thoughts and work. She wrote long letters to the Clark's, explaining everything and begging them not to be put off by her delayed plans. She was still returning. To prove her point, Meredith wrote two solid essays on the city of New Orleans upon hearing of the war's end. Meredith was with her own thoughts. She simply was not paying attention to the developments under her nose. That is until she did notice: then it struck her with considerable force. It was how Chardonnay looked at Liam and the manner in which he responded. As the late Billy Hunter would have said, they were lighting each other's candles.

Since the afternoon of his erection, Liam had become more circumspect around Chardonnay. He didn't want her to misconstrue his feelings. He was too late; she already knew, she could read him like a book and looked at him with such tenderness and love in her eyes, the likes of which he had never seen before. She was

151

a dear, dear girl. They both should fear for themselves the route they were going, but they didn't. Chardonnay cared little for the conventions of white folks; she had been brought up a slave, a house servant in training. For Liam, his reference to mixed racial romance was only a blur, maybe some sort of social stain. He was uncertain as there were no people of Chardonnay's race within miles of the farm where he was raised.

Yes, a sailor married a girl in the West Indies and brought her to live in town, but they only stayed a year or so. In the confederate south, black girls were for work and fun. That was all. He would not give his mother any possible complaint about what she would view as any sort of dalliance with a black girl. In Nova Scotia, there might be moral and social condemnations. He wanted to give his mother no excuse to launch a severe tongue lashing. Was there such a place Liam wondered, where races did not care about their differences? If so, he had never heard of it.

So, he dug down and tried to ignore his feelings for Chardonnay, his concern for her African race, her unidentified age, maybe ten years his junior. Besides his attraction to a young Negro woman, Liam was impacted by hidden things strangling him, like the grip of a dying man. Also, the thought of landing on his native shore made him tense, and every day he was getting closer. He desperately wanted to see his father and siblings, but his mother, well he ignored any thought of her, pushing hard to find some alternative to such worries.

Despite the hiding places on a ship, it is extremely difficult to hold a simple private conversation. Meredith and Chardonnay had their meals with the captain. Liam ate with the crew. There were always people around them. Finally, Meredith decided to hand Liam a note about her anxiety.

Dear Brother,

I am growing concerned that Chardonnay is becoming very attracted to you. Please remember she is a child and kindly limit your attention as she is unaccustomed to such tending as you shower upon her. Just a little reminder, dear brother. I do not want her hurt unnecessarily.

With great affection,

Your sister. M

She thought the note was too formal and wrote another but gave him the first one. They were brother and sister but not in the manner they once were. There was a formality between them, a certain ill-defined distance as if the war had blown a hole through their earlier relationship. They were, Meredith thought, strangers, trying to understand one another.

Liam responded within forty-eight hours. He had his own anxieties. One of which Meredith did not know.

Dearest Sister,

You will speak to me soon concerning Chardonnay. I know what is coming, I can see the look you give when Chardonnay laughs, and we enjoy each other. Indulge me, please. I am having a most difficult time with my problems, but I have successfully concealed any indication of ill health from you, but every day is a risk, and I am a nervous wreck. When it's terrible as it is terrible, some days, I make an excuse and hide in the head. I fear if we are up in the rigging when the affliction seizes me, I shall fall to my death. Thankfully it has not happened yet.

Not that I mind dying, but I certainly do not want to do so in front of my sister, the captain, or the beautiful Chardonnay. Is it immoral to love someone so young? Is it wrong to be so attracted to a woman of dark skin? It is my sincere hope that once home, the tension will lessen. It is hardly likely with mother yapping, but you are wise in telling them the whole truth the moment we get there. We leave in a month. Period. Let it sink in immediately. I know I am unwell; I know mother will see it immediately, maybe she will take pity. These shakes that come on me for two or three minutes every single day just at dusk - I know what they are. They beleaguer me at the very moment of the murder. Has the devil himself possessed me, or is it the soul of that lost soldier?

I would have written his kin had not the sergeant destroyed the letter we found on him. I would have asked them for forgiveness. There is a need in me to repent for my inability to correspond. I pray I can be healed. When I was a boy, I would stand at the very edge of our natural elevation, looking at the church steeples of the town. Birds flew below me. As a youth, I would wish I could spread my arms and fly or simply just fall. I feel that way in the rigging as our ship plunges into the troughs. They would think I slipped. My devastation comes at dusk. Chardonnay is a distraction, albeit a lovely one. When nightfall comes some night, you may no longer have to worry about this beautiful girl.

On their sixteenth day at sea just before dusk, the crew was called aloft, and Liam knew his fateful moment had come. He scurried up the ropes and was the first man up and therefore had to make his way to the very end of the boom where he pushed himself against it, his feet on only the rope, and he dangled there as he and his mates hauled up the forward sheets. The shaking started, and Liam fought to remain steady while the dead soldier's voice in his head told him to let go and be quick about it. The ship rocked and pitched in the growing darkness, and Liam McBurnie stayed alive.

Upon returning to the deck, his stomach muscles pained unmercifully. Liam had won a battle within himself or at least conquered a momentary skirmish. Chardonnay was waiting on deck. She knew the demons he was fighting. She gave him a look of total admiration, and he could feel things within him stirring. *"Oh, Dear God, deliver me from the temptations facing me. A child, a black girl, where could we ever be happy."* Then Liam laughed at himself bitterly. *"Happiness. What was that?"*

Five days later, they arrived in Halifax. The three of them took the train to Windsor and a ferry across the Minas Basin to Parrsboro where they hired a carriage to bring them up the hill home. Meredith could feel Liam's rigidity as they went up the steep grade to the farm.

"Maybe this was a mistake. Maybe I should have stayed lost. If you had not done as mother wanted and came looking for me..."

"What, Liam, you would stay hidden forever. Is that it? Well, let me tell you, if that were the case, our mother would have struck out searching for you herself or sent Jacob instead."

"Jacob would not have undertaken such a mission."

"Oh, why is that, is he smarter than me? Wiser than I am? I think he would have gone if for no other reason than just to get away."

Meredith spit her words rather than her usual careful enunciation, a clear indication that she was upset by his comment. It was not his intention to hurt her, but the truth stung. Jacob would not have gone on such a crazy mission.

"What were your plans before I found you? Meredith asked. *"Your intentions, did you plan never to reach out to your family again. Ever?"*

"What is the matter with you Meredith, I had no plans; there was never a Goddamn plan."

"Why are you swearing at me?" Why are you so disagreeable?"

Chardonnay touched Meredith on the arm. The man driving the wagon was listening. They should not be arguing minutes before they arrive at their parent's doorstep. It did not put them in the right spirit for such a monumental homecoming. It would be the biggest surprise of their parent's life, their two eldest children returning from the war. There were other things Meredith wanted to say, things that troubled her, particularly about Chardonnay. They had passed notes and talked about it once, or Meredith had talked, Liam had said nothing. It was not her age but her race, and Liam, *"Do you not see a problem?"*

The steep road up Kirk Hill rounded a corner at the top of the promontory and came upon the flat natural elevation, ran for two and a half miles, and held fourteen small farms, a one-room school, and a small clapboard church. Three of the farms were empty, the rest bare bones. The McBurnie spread was the first farm to be seen, nearest the sloping edge of the natural elevation. As their carriage rolled into the farmyard, Meredith saw two figures bending over a wagon wheel. Her father and Jacob. Her heart quickened. They were home.

Chapter 19

Liam jumped down and ran to his father, leaving Meredith to pay the driver. Meredith then flew into her father's arms as well. Already her brothers and sister were running from the farmhouse, excitedly laughing and yelping. Sarah was doing circles across the yard while looking towards the sky. Behind her was Vena, seeing what all the excitement was about and then running, surging into Liam and refusing to share him with the others.

How different papa looked, Meredith thought, so thin and pale. As for Clifton's part, he could not conceal his happiness as he repeatedly thanked Meredith for what she had done. Against all the odds, she had found him. *"Thank you..."* was all he could say. As she hugged him, Meredith could feel the hot tears on his cheek.

Jacob also took Meredith in his arms and hugged her and thanked her many times for coming home and bringing Liam.

"Maybe, we will have peace now," he whispered. Then Vena, finally releasing Liam, stiffly came up to Meredith almost hesitantly as if she was suddenly suspicious of this outpouring of happiness around her. *"Thank you, Meredith; I knew if anyone could find him, it would be you."* She gave her daughter a quick peck on the cheek and returned to Liam. It was only then that Meredith noticed Chardonnay still sitting in the carriage watching them with an expression that was impossible to translate. The driver was standing by the rig, ready to leave. He had offloaded everything they had brought and wanted to get back to town. Meredith took her father to Chardonnay. *"Daddy, this is my friend Chardonnay."*

Clifton McBurnie was not a man who concealed his feelings well. He was genuinely surprised to see a beautiful young negro girl. Jacob had just noticed her too.

There were no Africans around these parts, but Clifton didn't ask any questions. He shyly doffed his hat and said, *"Pleased to meet ya."*

Meredith tentatively approached her mother. *"Mother, I would like to introduce my friend from the United States. This is Chardonnay."*

"She is black," Vena said, taking a step back as if Chardonnay carried some contagion. More silence as they all stared at Chardonnay and Vena. Ignoring the rest of them, Vena turned again and hugged Liam. *"Son, I have prayed for you every single day."*

Then Liam made the unkind, cutting gesture. He formed a fist with his hand and slightly pushed it into his mother's chest moving her away from him.

"You should have saved your prayers, Momma. I am not the son you remember. The one you drove away. That boy is long dead."

Then he grabbed Chardonnay by the arm. *"Come, I want to show you my favorite place in all the world."* He yanked her away, and Chardonnay looked back at them with something like fright in her eyes. Meredith shouted to him, *"Liam, where are you taking her?"*

"To the glade, of course."

The others watched as Liam and Chardonnay disappeared into the nearby trees.

Liam's action had taken the air out of them. The only sound was Sarah's humming as she spun herself faster and faster until, out of dizziness, she fell down laughing. Meredith felt Percy's arms around her. *"Oh, Percy, you are so big."*

"Almost fourteen," Percy said as Cecil fell into Meredith's arms as well. Janet had finally left the house and joined them. She was a year younger than Meredith and already jilted by a young man who had run off to sea. She gave Meredith a slow nod but nothing more. No smile shaped her lips, no arms raised for a hug. There was something about her sister that told Meredith to keep her distance. Janet went and stood by her mother, who looked shaken and bewildered.

They went into the house, and Jacob, more handsome than ever, pulled out a chair for Meredith. Jacob, the twins, and Clifton did most of the talking. Still in abject shock by Liam's strange action, Vena sat stiffly, and Janet made tea. Meredith was uneasy. She had some important information to reveal and to tell it as quickly as possible. Yet, she found it difficult to talk about leaving when they had just arrived.

The oldest daughter, who, moments earlier, had returned in triumph with the prodigal son, was about to put a damper on things. *"Papa, we are only staying a month."*

They stopped talking. Vena, straightened, stiffened. Meredith knew the signs, as did the others. Janet was swiftly at her mother's side, steadying her as Vena was slightly swaying as if listening to some mysterious melody in her head.

"You are only staying one month!" Vena's eyes were burning, glaring at Meredith. She crooked her head as some reptiles do before striking. Then she spoke in a deep voice reserved only for occasions when her point of view would prevail.

"It took you long enough, months and months to find him, and now you are only staying with us a few weeks. Why?"

"Momma, please, they just arrived." Jacob spoke up while Janet whispered in her mother's ear, burying her face from the rest of the family. Clifton frowned but slowly nodded that he understood. Sarah was standing on her head in the corner by the wood box. She was unconcerned that her dress had fallen over her waist and her undergarments were in full display. In one of her long rambling letters, Vena had written about Sarah and how unconcerned she was about walking around "bare naked." Sarah was high on the list of her mother's troubles.

"She will run off with the first man who asks her and come back in a few years with a parcel of kids, and whose job will that be?" Meredith looked at her sister standing on her head and remembered that letter and Vena's comment about the "parcel of kids." Meredith got up and brought Sarah back to the table.

They all listened as Meredith told them of some of her adventures. She was uncomfortable, wishing Liam and Chardonnay would return, but glad Jacob had spoken up: a new ally. Jacob with a deeper voice and broader shoulders. Except for her mother, they had all changed in some manner. Jacob had filled out, the twins had grown taller, Clifton looked tired and thin, and Janet appeared withdrawn. Only Vena remained the same, always rail-thin and wiry. Meredith could not remember when her mother's face wasn't creased with the cares of life, and her tightly pulled back hair was gray and white.

But it was Jacob who had transformed the most. From her mother's letters, Meredith knew he was another one on Vena's Troubles List. Jacob had tasted love, run away with a town girl, but they did not get far. They took the coach to Springhill, but it was slow going because of the deep snow, and by the time they arrived, a dozen horsemen were waiting for them. It is easier to retrieve a son after a severe beating by a girl's hostile family who insists on keeping their daughters chaste until marriage. He was bloodied and bruised when Clifton picked up his battered and half-frozen son by the side of the road and put him gently in his farm wagon. They helped him to bed, and he had stayed there for three days. But Jacob would be on her side, Meredith felt. He was now old enough to speak up. Here she was at home only minutes and already thinking of sides. Them against her. Within the first half hour, Meredith felt the family dynamic beginning to reveal itself.

Finally, Liam and Chardonnay were back among them. Chardonnay looked uneasy and timid, but Liam seemed more relaxed as if the glade had refreshed him. He began talking to the twins, telling them about his adventures and the places he had been. His mother watched him closely with her eyes half-closed, her lips pressed tight, and her complexion chalk white. A bit of laughter began. Things were settling down when Vena said, *"Why did you run away from the army?"* Her voice cut through the fragile family merriment as if a five-pound cannonball had been fired through the kitchen. Things went dead again. Even poor addled Sarah sensed it. Liam looked at his mother, who showed no emotion on her face, and ignored the little pleas of, *"Mother, shhh, Momma, please."*

Liam gave his mother an icy stare. Meredith was now accustomed to the hard side of his nature. That persona of a killer, that frightening characteristic that kept bums away from them in the park in New Orleans; that aspect of him that bespoke of danger.

"I murdered a man Momma. I stabbed him through the heart. He lay dead in front of me like all those bodies on the battlefield of Fredericksburg, except we were alone. Him and me, you see, and I shoved a knife into him. That's why I left the Goddamn army."

Theirs was a Christian home, as Presbyterian as John Knox himself, and such oaths were never heard within its walls. There was stone silence only broken by Sarah's gasp, *"You swore, you took the name of the..."*

"That's enough, Sarah," Janet whisked her outside. Meredith looked at her mother, whose face suddenly held an odd, fearful expression. Meredith intervened.

"I have told Liam it was war, not murder, but he is taking it hard."

159

"Am I, Meredith? Is that what I am doing? Taking it hard."

"Why did you not write to us?" Vena asked, with less force than her previous question.

"Why." Liam said, *"because I was already dead and remain dead, that is why. My sister gave up so much, went through so much to find me. She will tell you of her suffering, the humiliation and pain she experienced."*

Meredith was shocked. She had no intention of ever revealing her shame to the family. Liam was doing it again. Making her the victim when in truth, he was the victim, the damaged one. Already transforming himself into the hero of his misadventure in front of his mother's cold stare.

Liam was going to California to try his luck there. Meredith and Chardonnay would be off to Portland. The news had been revealed, the family informed, and a quiet presence overcame the kitchen as they sipped their tea, and the twins asked Meredith what the wagon train was like. They dispersed then, Jacob and Clifton and Meredith taking Chardonnay to the edge of the promontory to show her the view. Liam tagged along behind, and Clifton tried to engage him in conversation. Then they took Chardonnay to the family cemetery where little Flora lay, along with baby Julie who fell victim to consumption many years back.

The next stumbling block to face the family concerned sleeping arrangements. When Meredith said Chardonnay could sleep with her and Janet, both sister and mother were taken aback.

"She cannot."

Chardonnay physically withered at that remark, whispering to Meredith that she would sleep in the barn. *"No, you will not."* She pressed Chardonnay to her as she said to Vena, *"Momma, Chardonnay and I have been sleeping together for months now."* Before she could continue, her mother turned her back to her.

Janet, now seventeen years and tall like Meredith, was more adamant. *"Meredith, I am not sleeping with a black woman. You can if you choose, but I cannot."*

"Enjoy yourself in the barn then," Meredith replied, too quickly without thinking. The family was bringing out the worst in her. Meredith bit her lip, but her patience was already exhausted.

"When did you become so high and mighty, Janet? Chardonnay is my friend. We have been through a lot together."

Janet pushed back her shoulders and took a step towards her sister. *"Well, we have been through a lot too, Meredith. Have you considered that?"*

"Have you Janet? What did you go through? Slip in the mud in the farmyard? Is that what you have been through?"

"I have had to put up with Sarah and mother. Work, work, work and care for, care for, care for."

"I have done that for years myself," Meredith replied. *"Have you spent weeks on a wagon train? Could you even imagine how uncomfortable that is? Did you experience the murder and mutilation of a friend? Were you dragged by the hair of your head by a man on horseback? Did you witness the stabbing and murder of a friend? What exactly are your hardships?"* Meredith had said more than she wanted, more than she planned.

"You do not understand," said Janet, walking away.

"If you don't like farm work, don't marry a farmer."

Janet turned, mouth agape. *"How did you know?"* Meredith, until that moment, did not know, but things were not going as she had hoped.

In the days that followed, the family took on some new characteristics. Certainly, Chardonnay and the attention showered on her by the older brothers altered the family chemistry. Chardonnay was accepted by the men in the family. Even Percy and Cecil, somewhat shy, were polite and friendly, and Clifton was his usual lovable self.

Only damaged Sarah could not stop pestering Chardonnay as to why she had black skin and - "not skin like us."

Chardonnay was told the truth. Sarah was not right in the head; was how it was put. Hadn't been since she and Flora were struck by lightning. Sarah stuck close to Chardonnay until a frustrated Liam would shoo her away. Jacob wanted to spend time with his brother and Chardonnay too, but farm work called him away. Then there was the Sunday morning service, and once more, things came to a head. Vena took Meredith aside.

"I want you all to come to church. That Negro girl will have to stay here."

"Momma, her name is Chardonnay."

"Yes, well, whatever her name is, she must remain here."

"Whatever for?"

"I want my family with me; she is not my family. She will remain here."

"Then I will remain here also."

"No, you will not. I want you with us."

"You will not get your wish Momma, I will not leave her alone in this house while we go and ask God for forgiveness and our daily bread."

"What is that girl to you? She is not family." It was her mother's familiar snarl, and Meredith was determined not to shrink from it as she had done in her youth.

"For most of the past year, Momma, she has been the only family I have had. She found me." Meredith stopped. She would not say more, would never reveal her inner disgrace: the awful truth that she would never marry as a virgin. Her mother would not know the hell she had been through.

Clifton intervened, and he did so forcefully. Meredith had never seen her father so adamant, and Vena, her jaw locked tightly, left the room. Clifton was winded and slumped into a chair. He was breathing deeply while offering Meredith a weak smile.

Chardonnay accompanied the McBurnie family to the little church that served up spiritual nourishment to the inhabitants of surrounding farms. The local girls were delighted to see both Liam and Jacob in attendance while their parents whispered about the return of Clifton's son and daughter and the young woman with them. *"Meredith has brought her back from the Boston states. She has a high position there; she writes with the likes of Longfellow,"* Vena stated.

Meredith began looking for passage. She took Chardonnay to town with her just to whisk her away from the grasp of Liam. Many townsfolk stared at the beautiful young woman, and old sailors relived their youthful prime in the West Indies.

Meredith was spending as much time as possible with her father, and she was disappointed Liam was not. His time was devoted to Chardonnay, and Jacob alternated between them and the chores at hand. It worried Meredith how Liam and Chardonnay would go off by themselves for hours at a time. She could occasionally hear the sweet chords of his flute floating from the glade.

"Liam takes me everywhere," Chardonnay told her that night. *"We go to the end of the farm where you can look down and see the church steeples of the town. He takes me to the woods and draws my picture."* She had three of his sketches of herself. One Meredith had noticed was of Chardonnay with bare shoulders. Liam had been busy. Busy with Chardonnay but not with anyone else. He and his mother hardly had spoken since his outburst, and when Vena attempted a conversation, he either shut up or walked away. Janet was moody and distant to all of them. *"What was going on with that girl?"* Meredith asked her father. Clifton shook his head in despair and mopped his brow, *"Janet got jilted, a young man courted her and skipped off to sea after promises were made and never kept. Now she sees a young farmer, but I do not think he is for her. She is full of despair."*

"Oh papa, you have such a time with your children," Meredith said, hugging him. Clifton, Jacob, and the twins, Cecil and Percy, were themselves, but Vena had gone strangely silent, always asking where Liam was and always snarly when told he was off with... "that girl," as Janet put it. At the beginning of their third week, an event happened that changed the atmosphere on the farm. Almost against his will, Liam was held captive in the kitchen with a thousand questions peppered in quick succession by his mother. It gave Chardonnay an opportunity to be in the farmyard with Jacob as he was hitching the horse and wagon for town. Chardonnay told Meredith she was invited to go along. When Liam discovered his brother and Chardonnay had gone to town, he flew into an incredible rage, accusing Meredith of plotting against him. He was beside himself. Irritable, half-mad, snarling, he told Meredith she had no right to let Chardonnay go off with Jacob.

"What right have you over her? I am booking passage for myself and Chardonnay as soon as I can."

"You can leave her with me," he said, giving Meredith an extremely hateful expression. At one time, she could read his face like an open book. Now he was virtually impossible to comprehend.

"I shall do no such thing. She is coming with me."

"We will see," Liam said.

"Stop acting like a love-sick puppy. What is wrong with Chardonnay going off with Jacob? For Pete's sake, Liam, you are not a child."

"You dragged me back here. You know my feeling for Chardonnay. Jacob is trying to horn in on me, and you are willing to let that happen."

"First of all, Liam, are you prepared to stand against your race and the prejudice therein to take her as your wife, or are you just using her for your own amusement?" She had to go on: there was no stopping at that point. *"You said you wanted to spend time with papa, but you hardly have said two words to him or Momma. You are always going off with Chardonnay. She is not why you are here."*

He went wild-eyed. *"I will not have you telling me how to live my life. Go back to Maine by yourself."*

"Chardonnay is coming with me."

"Maybe she is, maybe not."

"Oh no, Liam, she is most definitely coming with me."

"We'll see," he said and walked away.

His talk alarmed Meredith. Everything about him frightened her. He seemed dangerous in some new way she did not understand. But at that moment, she was sure of one thing. She and Chardonnay would leave Nova Scotia as soon as possible.

It was high noon when Clifton's wagon came back up the hill and into the farmyard. Jacob had hardly helped Chardonnay to the ground when Liam flew at him, wildly punching his brother. After receiving two or three solid blows, Jacob started hitting back. Clifton, coming out of the barn, tried to intervene. Is there any scene more pathetic than a frail father in the middle of two sons in fisticuffs? With considerable effort and very heavy breathing, Clifton separated his boys but not before getting knocked to the ground. Vena ran out of the house shrieking at them, holding her broom and fiercely pounding both her sons. Chardonnay ran into the house, and as she did, Liam screeched at her to stay away from Jacob.

"Are you crazy," Vena, in turn, screamed at Liam in her high-pitched shriek. *"You will have nothing to do with that negro woman. Do you understand me? Both of you, stay away from that woman."*

Vena turned then, pointing that hateful, crooked, accusing finger directly into Meredith's face. *"This is your doing. You brought her here."*

"Yes, I did, Momma, and I am going to take her away from here as fast as I can."

"Please," Clifton spoke in a wobbly voice getting to his feet. *"Please do not fight."*

THE END OF DREAMS

With those words of pleading to his family for peace, Clifton McBurnie, the patriarch of the clan McBurnie, fell over dead in the farmyard.

Chapter 20

Before the dreadful day was done, Janet would accuse Meredith of killing their father. The first hours after Clifton died in the dirt of his farmyard were difficult to explain or even remember as the family completely broke down. Vena refused to look at her dead husband, saying aloud he was not dead but merely sleeping. *"Leave him alone,"* she ordered and refused to do anything but walk across the fields to the little cemetery where dear Flora and Julie were buried and where her husband of many years would soon join his daughters.

Chardonnay was bitterly crying in her room. *"What is happening Miss Meredith? Why is everybody so angry? Why is Liam being mean to your mother? Why did you bring me here? When Jacob tries to be nice to me, Liam gets mad. I do not understand your family. Many white people do not like slaves around. I have been chased off people's farms before. But you have been so kind. I thought your family would be like you. But they are not. Your daddy is dead, and they blame me. But I did not want him to die. He and Jacob have been so nice, and Liam, I do not understand what is happening to him."*

"Neither do I Chardonnay. Neither do I. None of this is your fault."

They had the bedroom to themselves; Janet had been sleeping with her parents since the day they arrived, and she was mighty upset about it too. Meredith sat down on the bed and let her emotions go. It was too much. She shook her head in disbelief. *"All the hardship, all the searching and wretched experiences I've been through to bring my family together. It is truly heartbreaking."*

Meredith broke down and cried, and she and Chardonnay strongly embraced and wept together. But Chardonnay had not finished her lament. She confided that Liam was beginning to really frighten her. He was possessive, and she had told Jacob of her fears that morning in town. Meredith felt the full weight of her family fall upon her shoulders.

Downstairs a hostile Janet was throwing pots around the kitchen. A bewildered Jacob who, against his mother's wishes, had carried his father's body into the house, now sat with the heartbroken twins weeping out of sight in the hayloft. Sarah did circles in the parlor until Meredith rushed her outside. Liam had immediately gone off to the glade and inappropriately played jigs on his flute. Hour after hour, he played, despite Meredith pleading with him to stop. As the neighbors came to prepare Clifton's body for burial, they could hear hornpipes and jigs coming from the glade.

How crazy these good neighbors think we are, Meredith thought. She had had enough. Marching to the glade for the third time to request Liam to stop his music and show respect, the brother and sister confronted each other with new bitterness and hostility and more hurtful words than ever before existed between them. Where once they had sat and talked, they now hurled accusing barbs and insults that led to Liam producing a pistol from his belt and pressing it hard against his temple. *"Liam, what are you doing?"*

"I am dead to you Meredith, dead to you all. I have been dead for a long time. It is only Chardonnay that breathes any life into me. Leave me be with her and go to Maine, do what you want to do, live your own life."

"There has been too much misery in finding you to just forget you. You are my brother, and I love you." Meredith grabbed the pistol out of Liam's hand and would not give it back to him. It led to the most serious confrontation where Liam called her a wretched bitch and whore and informed her that he was taking Chardonnay.

"I am not a whore, but I know whores. I met them while I was looking for you. You thoughtless bastard who could not communicate with his parents. I would not leave Chardonnay with you under any circumstances."

"It is me or nobody ever," he screamed and demanded the pistol be returned to him immediately.

"Give me the pistol or give me Chardonnay. You cannot keep both."

Meredith, sick at heart, walked back to the house and hid the pistol in the barn. Liam had scared her. Scared her for what he said, the threatening, awful words and the expression of hostility, but mostly it was the hatred in his eyes. Meredith felt her heart was breaking. She returned to the house and walked over pots and pans Janet had thrown on the floor. Meredith hitched the family farm wagon and moved with Chardonnay taking their limited possessions to town. Clifton had a sister there. They would return for the funeral, and that was all, leaving behind a broken family that she had tried so desperately to put back together.

Chapter 21

Clifton's funeral fell on the hottest day of the season. The McBurnie farmyard filled up with carriages and wagons as neighbors and friends came to pay their final respects. The group of about thirty walked over the fields to the little cemetery. Jacob, Cecil, and Percy were among the pallbearers carrying the wooden box that Clifton had made a few years ago for the day it would be needed. At the graveside, there were phrases from the Old Testament, picked by Vena, that spoke of polluting a home with unclean things. Meredith felt every reading was pointed at her. It was expedient that they leave as soon as possible. Liam was acting more and more bizarre. Meanwhile, Jacob was prepared to be Chardonnay's protector and told her so in front of his mother and brothers. If necessary, he would protect her from Liam.

Meredith could book passage within a fortnight. She then went to visit the presbyterian minister who had performed the funeral service. Meredith knew she needed help; she told the pastor her entire story and pleaded for assistance with her family that had so severely fallen apart.

"My mother says this is my doing because I brought a beautiful young woman here and and..."

"The young woman of color," the pastor said. "Liam cannot have her. You cannot mix races, you know. It is forbidden."

Meredith got up and left him there. Everything was forbidden to Presbyterians.

Upon returning to her aunt's house where they were staying, she immediately sensed something was wrong. Her Aunt Helen was outside, frantically waving at her.

169

"He took her; Liam did. He barged in here and took her." Aunt Helen, Clifton's oldest sister, was breathless, panting and trying not to choke on her words. *"Liam pushed me aside, just shoved me out of the way, and your friend did not want to go. She struggled. He picked her up like a sack of flour and put her over the horse and rode off."*

Meredith stopped and asked people if they had seen Liam riding by. She was certain Liam had taken Chardonnay back to the farm. Aunt Helen's horse was old and could not run fast and was in a sweat before reaching the bottom of the elevation. The animal was drawing deep breaths going up the grade, but even over the hoof beats on the rocks and rapid breathing of the winded animal, Meredith could hear the far-off sound of women crying. Then the sudden bone-chilling howl of her mother. The horse stumbled, and the heart of Meredith McBurnie was breaking over the rattling ululation of her mother. What was happening? Meredith drove into a scene of absolute turmoil. Jacob was lying on the ground covered in blood. His mother and Janet were bending over him, trying to stop the bleeding. Percy and Cecil were standing close by, their faces chalk white. Upon seeing Meredith, Jacob tried to raise himself but could not get to his feet.

"What happened?" Meredith shrieked, although deep down, she already knew what had transpired.

"He was treating her rough, Meredith," Jacob said in a throaty whisper, *"I tried to stop him, but he stuck me."*

"Liam did this," Vena shrieked, *"with the pitchfork. It's all over that girl you brought here. This is all your fault."*

"You spend so much time, Momma, trying to figure out who is to blame. Maybe you and your craziness are to blame. Did you ever think of that?"

"I'm alright," Jacob said, *"I'll be fine, it's not deep, but it sure hurts."*

"You need a doctor; Meredith, get on that wagon and rush to town and fetch Dr. MacDonald."

"No, you and Janet take him. I must find Chardonnay. Where is she?"

"You place that girl before your own brother?" Vena's voice was as shrill as the snap of a whip. Her eyes were flaming, her hands shaking as if she was coming apart in front of her children.

"Where did he take her Momma, where?"

"I don't know and care less. Help your brother, never mind Liam."

"No, he may hurt her. Where did he take her?"

Then, wafting out of the woods, Meredith heard the familiar notes of the flute. The glade, his favorite place. Meredith rose quickly. She raced into the barn, retrieved the pistol, and ran to the wooded area through the fields. She tore down the path into the glen, where they spent the few leisure hours that farm kids have in their childhoods. The glade was empty. Meredith looked up and down the brook. The little stream ran off the nearby mountain range and ambled through open fields where they picked wild blueberries as children. Many years ago, Clifton had banked off half of the brook to make a pool for the children to swim in and wash. Meredith raced along the brook, brushing by ferns and swatting pine branches and alders from her face. Rounding the bend, she saw Chardonnay floating face down in the pool. Meredith issued a whimpering cry, the sound of a wounded animal as she plunged into the cold water. She took the dear limp body in her arms and pressed it to her bosom.

"I told her," Liam's voice was near. It was raspy and tortured somewhere above her. He was standing on one of the boulders above the stream. *"I told her Meredith, I told her." It was me, or it was nobody. She would not listen. Not listen to reason. I told her."*

Clutching her dear dead friend tightly, her almost-daughter, holding her close and fast in her arms, Meredith stood watching her mad brother ramble on. Slowly walking out of the pool, she gently placed Chardonnay on the soft ground. Then Meredith McBurnie straightened up, took the small revolver from her pocket, and pointed it at Liam. She didn't take careful aim. She just pointed through her hot tears and fired.

She killed him. Meredith knew it immediately the way blood blew out of him when his head exploded. She threw the gun into the pool, again lifted Chardonnay in her arms, and began her return to the house. As she walked, she sobbed aloud deliriously. *"My beautiful daughter will be buried here. We have the room. A family cemetery big enough for twenty is what they called it when papa built it when little Flora died. Chardonnay has never had a real home; this will be her home forever and ever. This is the least I can do for her."*

As the farmhouse came into view, Meredith saw her mother standing at the door watching her.

The End

Epilogue

Meredith McBurnie was arrested for the murder of Liam McBurnie. After hearing the entire story, told mainly by Jacob, the jury refused to convict her of anything but manslaughter. She was sentenced to five years in the women's penitentiary in Kingston Ontario. My father and Cecil dug the graves for Liam and Chardonnay. The sound of shovels chipping rocks mingled with tearful sobs of the teenage twins. As they dug Liam's grave, Vena wept and shook her fists at God, demanding his immediate appearance: she wanted to have it out with him. For hours she circled the little cemetery, her face towards the sky as she waited for some divine deliverance. Sarah began to imitate her mother, and as the two brothers dug and sobbed, their mother and sister walked for hours with faces pointed toward the sky, each, in turn, yelling into the heavens. God did not come. With Meredith taken away by the sheriff, Janet and Vena had a free hand and refused to bury Chardonnay in the family plot. Strangely Chardonnay was buried in the glade.

Vena died a few weeks later, seized by a massive stroke only feet from where her husband had fallen. Sarah was carried off by the pox a year after Meredith was released from penitentiary. Cecil was killed in the Boar War and Percy, succumbed to influenza in 1918.

Because she was a convicted felon, Meredith McBurnie could never return to the United States and never wrote another word to the best of my knowledge. She and Janet scraped together what they could and ran the farm until they were very old ladies. Meredith McBurnie died in 1933 at the age of eighty-seven. She outlived Janet by seven years and is buried next to Chardonnay in the glade. Meredith managed to save enough funds for a small headstone for Chardonnay. It read:

BRUCE GRAHAM

Chardonnay
A Beloved Daughter.

About the Author

Bruce Graham is a Canadian writer, poet, and playwright. He is the author of eleven books and several short stories. Three of his books have been transformed into stage plays. Bruce's writing falls into two broad categories: historical fiction and humor. His characters are based on people from his childhood and have been set in and around his hometown of Parrsboro, Nova Scotia.

Before becoming a writer, Bruce had a long and illustrious career in broadcasting. Bruce is an honors graduate of the Radio and Television Arts program of Cambridge School in Boston. His work in broadcasting has earned him three prestigious awards, including a Lifetime Achievement Award from the Canadian Radio & Television News Directors Association, the Ohio State Award for journalistic excellence, and an Atlantic Journalism Award for his nightly television commentary, "The Final Word".

Bruce lives in picturesque Cumberland County, Nova Scotia, with his wife Helen. Along with writing poetry, Bruce enjoys gardening, reading, and theatre.

Other Works